VIVA NOTHING

Viva Nothing
by Rick Rien

ЯR

First published in Great Britain 2023
Copyright © Rick Rien 2023
135798642

ISBN 9780956781154

For all enquiries, please contact
rickrienbooks@gmail.com

Typeset in 11.5/14pt Granjon LT Std
by Joke De Winter Graphic Design

Image on cover by Rick Rien

Printed and bound in Great Britain
by Clays Ltd, Elcograf S.p.A.

I drove up to Chiswick on Saturday morning to have lunch at a friend's place, arriving half an hour early to place a few bets at the bookies across the green.

Sitting down to eat I wondered how the match was going and slyly checked on the phone. Man City were already one up after seven minutes.

Arsenal had lost the first two games of the season, our worst start for over forty years. Man City had spluttered too and the day before they'd missed out on signing Ronaldo to United. I had fifty on Arsenal to win at 10/1. The other three bets of twenty apiece were pure whimsy; two defenders, neither of whom had ever scored for the Gunners, to score first at silly odds, and Aubameyang to score a hat-trick at 400/1.

By the time lunch was over we were three-nil down and it wasn't even half-time. All my bets would lose but it was only a shade over a hundred quid. Just a day's wages if I was working for another painter. Manageable.

I couldn't engage with my friend, never can when a bet's on. It's incredibly rude and off-putting, and goes a long way to explain why I have so few friends. Gambling always comes first.

I needed to put the record straight and return to the bookies. It was the only solution. I'd have to get tanked up on a few lagers beforehand and I knew which pub to go to, right across the green and only a few minutes' walk from the bookies. I was salivating at the prospect. If I stayed I'd miss the second half at the pub.

In the end, I feigned not feeling well and left. Very poor behaviour.

There were only two other blokes in the pub so I quickly ordered my first pint and stood at the bar to watch the match. Just as I got another one in, City scored an easy fourth. Aubameyang had been taken off so all my bets were duds.

I went outside for a roll up and drank greedily. Back inside, City put away a fifth just as I ordered another pint. Drinking into it, registering the loss, the flavour for a flutter was well and truly on. That third pint is decisive.

Downing it quickly I walked off to the bookies with sparks flying across my brain.

I worried that my friend might see me (she was going somewhere in a taxi after lunch) but there wasn't much I could do about that. I've lost a lot of money in the last few weeks and my need to straighten things out has gone haywire. I would say I've lost all sense of dignity due to my gambling.

Installed at the bookies, with a virtual race going off in fifty seconds, I got my first two bets on. I have a fair amount of luck with virtual races by picking the names of virtual horses that I think no one else will side with. I went for Atomic Austrian at 11/1, and Snurge at tens. Atomic won and Snurge placed. I always go for the place on virtuals and I'd put a tenner each-way on the pair of them, my earlier losses recouped with a little splash on top to play with.

From there, I started my idiotic odyssey, knowing full well I'd only stop if I was a grand up (which hardly ever happens) or I lost the lot. I had about twelve hundred quid.

The trouble with me and gambling is that one part of my brain tells me I can stop when I'm maybe a few hundred up, that I can go back to the pub, have a pint and trundle off home. The other part says carry on and be bold. Strike with the luck. Go for the grand.

The feverish buzz from the pints always tells me to carry on, which I suppose is why I get tanked up. I love the desperate devil may care freefall feeling of being in the lap of the horse Gods. After about half an hour the buzz tapers off and I need more alcohol, or is it sugar?

Luckily The Lamb is even closer than the footy pub so after a flurry of bets, mostly duds, I went and drained a quick pint to get the buzz back. Like all pleasures, it's never as good as the first.

Returning to the bookies the apprentice server shyly announced that he'd overpaid me by twenty quid on an earlier bet (he'd taken a twenty bet and in the heat of the moment forgotten to subtract it from another bet that I'd won a bit on). At the time, I thought of telling him but laziness, and greed, told me not to, which is always a bad omen for later bets.

When he asked for it back I returned it without fuss. The young manageress cast a beady eye my way but I flung it off and carried on with my silly odyssey, striking bets of anything from twenty to fifty quid every three or four minutes, shuffling between newspapers on walls.

One in two were coming in as each-ways but my bigger bets weren't winning. After about an hour I was still in the game, only a couple of hundred down, so I went back to The Lamb for another sharpener and looked on the phone for some horse names that took my fancy or made me laugh.

Back at the bookies I was in that otherworldly state of flux, resigned to lumping large on a horse. My wallet was pounding at my thigh.

Sticking two hundred on the nose of Fussmaker, a 3/1 favourite in an open eight-horse race at Newmarket, blood exploded into my face as Fussmaker plodded home last. With the war chest severely dented, I swore violently at the screen.

The servers knew how to take my bets, quickly, but their manner had changed. They probably thought I tried to stick him earlier but he'd made the mistake, not me.

Still, my bets were taken quickly and there were only a few other losers in the place. I didn't need to worry about getting flustered. Like most bad gamblers, I need a clean path to the counter for snap decision bets seconds before the off.

Of the eight hundred in cash, I had about four hundred left. I didn't want to use any of the four hundred in the bank because I had council tax and water to pay in the coming week plus I was doing my books with the new accountant the following weekend and she'd need paying.

The fear started to take hold but I batted it off with lots of spent lager bravado, senselessly staking twenty quid each-way bets every few minutes. Some placed but still no winners so I lumped large on a five-horse affair at Navan and finally my prayers were answered, winning three hundred to get me back in the game. I'd started to get slovenly, though, whistling like an idiot and swearing when my horses were pipped at the post or just plain ridden. I was getting on the nerves of the two old boys who were playing at the machines with peanuts but I couldn't let that bother me. Switching back to a virtual race after noticing a particularly funny horse name, it came stone last.

In no time at all, the wallet had thinned down to two lonely fifties, which were quickly dispatched on loser horses. I found a twenty in a back pocket, stuck it in a machine and after a minute I was sixty quid up so I took the chit and put it all on an outsider at Cartmel but it refused at the first hurdle, just stood there with the jockey booting him in the ribs.

Back at The Lamb I drained a pint and looked online at the next race at Beverley. There were two horses I fancied the names of so I went bowling back and put thirty-seven pound fifty each-way on both, totaling one-fifty, which I had to use the card on.

I needed a slash. The good thing about bookies in the posher parts of London is they usually have a decent toilet and sometimes a disabled one. This one had just a disabled one so

I went in there. The door's always open for easy access. It's a really quick piss and I never put the loo seat up because it won't stay up and they never use it anyway, plus I'm extra careful, not a spot.

Bookies in poor areas always have toilet problems, mostly because of the threat of drug use. If it's actually in working order, chances are it's the worst toilet you've been to. You have to heave in a load of air on entry and then hold your breath as you piss, the stench itching to get under your skin. It's a horrible experience but worse is when they're out of order. My bets go wrong when I've got a tummy full on board. The main thing about the bookies in the posh areas is you're not made to feel like a complete tool, or criminal, or plain nobody.

I'd like to take photos of bookies toilets and put them together in a booklet. It would be called 'Best Bookies Bogs'. At one particular place, the toilet was out of order for three weeks. The reason? I got it out of the server after a while - someone had done a king curly in the middle of the floor and a toilet technician from Newcastle had failed to attend due to illness. I think it may have been a joke but you never know these days.

By the time I got back to the screens both my horses were struggling at the rear of the pack. One was having the shit whipped out of its arse. The jockey on the other nag had given up. At the line the horse I'd had a feeling about (but didn't back) was being eased down with the post in sight, the best of the rest a good ten lengths behind.

I tried to hide a deep sense of loss with a sigh but it came out as an awkward cough, then I sneezed violently and the old boys carted their automatic wheelchairs over to the door, scared that they'd catch something chronic off me. I tried to tell them it was down to the air conditioning but they weren't having it. Just shook their heads. Anyone would have thought I'd thrown a stink bomb in there.

They always have the air con on at bookies for some reason

and they never turn it off so I don't bother asking anymore. I just stand out of the way of the downwind. I do wonder if they put oxygen and stuff in there like they do in the Vegas casinos. The way things are going I wouldn't be surprised if they stuck a bit of nerve gas in it.

With only two hundred and fifty odd quid left in the account I made that last gasp decision. What to do? Fight on or fuck off? I put a ton each-way on something at Wolverhampton and it came nowhere.

Fifty left. Completely screwed. No way back.

On the Tuesday of the week just gone, I had one of my wobbles after getting paid a grand in cash from a job. Finishing up just before midday, I went to a nice country pub and got myself fuelled up. Looking online for runners and riders I spotted a very weird horse name that made me laugh so much I got back in the car and zoomed off to a pub that's close to a half-decent bookies.

After a couple of very swift pints I trotted off to the bookies and lumped large on the funny named horse, which I can't remember now. It lost by a neck to a rank outsider.

I went even larger on some other nag in the next race and again it was pipped at the post, this time on the nod. My third roll in the hay with the devil saw my horse stumble at the last hurdle as it led by a good six lengths. The jockey lost his footing and the favourite sauntered past to kiss him at the death.

Just like in Chiswick, I'd looked in my wallet and found two lonely fifties, then a scraggly twenty in a back pocket. Desperate measures were required after screwing a week's wages in an afternoon.

I thought about what was in the fridge back at the flat. I could see the tub of mayonnaise, the old dates, the half pint of milk and various other odds and sods. There were the two remaining tins of tuna and some pasta in a cupboard but that was about it. I squeezed the pouch of tobacco in my pocket, almost empty.

If I put fifty each-way on something I'd still have just enough for another pouch.

I've always had terrible luck at Wincanton but it was the last race of the day and I wasn't about to walk away with a measly ton.

It was a six-horse affair with a firm odds-on favourite, three other nags all stood at around 4/1, with paltry prize money of about what I'd just blown.

The wacky outsider was Bold Medic. It had just changed hands and gone to a trainer with a good reputation for breathing life back into horses on long losing runs. Bold Medic hadn't won for over two years but, there at Wincanton, he'd come in from 25/1 in the morning down to 12/1 at starting price. That was reason enough for me to write the chit and place the fifty each-way bet.

Right at the off, the jockey of the favourite pushed firmly at its neck to get it going. Moments later it received another stern early reminder, this time with the whip. That had me licking my lips.

Bold Medic was in orange so he was easy to spot from the pack that had developed with maybe two lengths between them, once the favourite got back into the mix.

It was two miles and six furlongs so I stood there with my eyes fixed to the screen for any signs of my little baby faltering at fences.

Bold Medic held his position well. He looked good, just behind the leaders, skulking. Even the commentator noted how well settled he looked. One of the leading horses flapped and began to fall away from the pack. He had the shit whipped out of him for a while but then the jockey gave up. One down, four to go.

With two fences left, Bold Medic was still being held up, confidently ridden, but that could never be a sign of supremacy until buttons needed pressing and horsepower kicked in.

Only then would it be known what was left in the tank.

Just before jumping at the penultimate fence, Bold Medic's jockey offered a little nudge on his neck and he responded well, drawing closer to the leading pack on landing. Two other nags began to struggle.

At the final fence it came down to the odds-on favourite, a flagging nag and Bold Medic to battle out the short run in, each being whipped to shit with a short furlong to go.

I tried closing my eyes but that didn't work. I quietly prayed to God (come on God, show me you love me). Bold Medic drew alongside the favourite and the other nag fell away.

The three previous races flashed through my mind, all my horses' noses kissed at the death. But then, with the post in sight, Bold Medic found more and lunged ahead. The favourite found nothing and all I can remember is the deep orange of Bold Medic crossing the line in first place.

That gave me a sure win of eight hundred and fifty quid so I took a second to enjoy the buzz, then I noticed that the American races were starting up. I still had twenty quid on me so I stuck it on the nose of a 4/1 shot called Go Babyface Go. I can still hear the raucous commentator calling its name as it flew home unchallenged, another ton in the bag.

The server told me it would take a few minutes for the safe to unlock so I went outside and had a roll up to count the takings for the day. Including the pints and the crab salad at the country pub I was a whole tenner down.

Bold Medic was the only reason I still had eight hundred quid in my wallet that Saturday in Chiswick, and as I walked out of the bookies with my tail between my legs the only consolation from losing over a grand was that Bold Medic had made it a free ride. If he hadn't won I'd have still been betting but, crucially, only with peanuts. I wouldn't have had anything like the rollercoaster ride I'd been on.

I went back to the footy pub for a quick pint, to find my

bearings before driving home. The Liverpool v Chelsea game was on and little groups of people were perched on stools like alien pods. I grabbed my pint and walked outside for a roll up.

That day, I'd placed bets to the value of about five or six grand, winning a few big ones, losing a load and clawing back a whole host of each-ways. The virtuals had cost me dear after my initial win with Atomic Austrian but it couldn't be helped. I took one peek into the wallet and found a scraggly tenner, then I dug my hand into my pocket and grabbed at change blind. Maybe another twenty. I'd left fifty-seven quid in the account so I wasn't going to starve over the bank holiday weekend. With all the confusion, my throat throbbed as my heartbeat rose and the blood struggled in my brain.

Sat at a bench, a bearded hipster was talking to someone on the phone about The Great Fire of London and I remembered a friend posting something about how traffic in Hackney had been brought to a standstill because of some mad experiment post the restrictions. He'd videoed a massive tailback with an ambulance stood still for fifteen minutes.

The councils have started ticketing anyone who goes onto side streets in a push to allow residents some peace but it's really a way to increase revenue with congestion and emissions as its excuse and motivator. It's a sad state of affairs when an ambulance can't get past a jam. The main roads now have cycles lanes, which are also bus lanes, to give Londoners a smoke-free town, buses and cars and trucks chugging out the fumes, all idling in the road together. With the system clogged to shit and traffic moving at a snail's pace it's worse than counterproductive, but so long as the cameras work and tickets are being issued, it's easy streets for the council.

The world's a mess. The East End, with its plague and its great fire and its abject indigenous poverty, is still the same, Dickensian, awash with those who serve London. Right now, what with everything that's going on, it feels like The Great

Fire of London all over again, only without the fire. This time it's invisible smog.

It was almost dusk outside that pub. I looked across the road to Turnham Green and saw a father and son kicking a football together in acres of space. Yes, the cycle lanes were there and vehicle lanes had been narrowed but there was no congestion, not in leafy west London. People were drawing up on single yellows in flash cars to nip into Waitrose and I saw a woman stagger out of a Porsche and come back a few minutes later with bottles clunking about in a bag. I'm a fine one to talk and I know what you're thinking, having totted up my quota for the day, but don't forget I'd just spent the best part of five hours in the office (that's the bookies to you). However stupid I am my mind's as sharp as a pin and I don't do falling out of cars and staggering about. If you want to stay in the game these days you have to be well on the ball. An old friend once told me, if someone gets sent to prison it's because they want to go. They've just plain had enough of freedom.

It's true I'd just lost eleven hundred quid but I'd be dead by now if I let that get to me. All I know is I'm a pathological gambler who refuses to learn lessons. I've made so many mistakes that they've become the norm. Life's a survival course between binges. I'm constantly jumping off cliffs.

I finished off the pint and walked across the green down past my friend's house, hoping she wouldn't see me.

The drive home was crap. The A4 has had its road signs taken down because they're turning that and the M4 into a superhighway with no hard shoulder in accordance with the previously projected increase in traffic, which will now never materialize.

I was listening to a Best of Lennon CD and missed the turn for the M25 so I had to go to the next junction, also unmarked, and turn back. When I got onto the A3 I started thinking about having one more somewhere but being broke and wondering how I could make eighty quid last till Wednesday was enough to get me straight home. I'd filled the tank on the way up but I hadn't been to the supermarket since Tuesday. I'd scrape by. All I really needed was a pack of roll ups and a tin of undercoat for the job starting Tuesday, which would then pay the bills and the accountant.

I batted away the dark thoughts about how much I'd lost and what a crap dad I am, how I'd never see my kids again and probably for good reason. They were better off without me. I've been twelve years a ghost to them.

It must have been about nine by the time I got home. I put something together and had it with toast and butter, then watched some footy on the telly. In a moment of weakness I almost sent a text to the lady asking her to let me have some of the money she's been looking after for me. It was a close call because I'd written the text and even lied that I'd found a van to buy and needed to pay for it the next day, knowing I'd gamble with it over the bank holiday weekend. That's how my brain works. It tells me I'll have a gargantuan amount of luck and win big and fuck off to France and buy a flat in a sleepy village and do it up so I can die there and leave it to my kids, but it never happens.

All I do is bet whimsically, pissed or not, imagining that Lady Luck's with me, just that once. The truth is I'm a hardened loser with no real knowledge of racing. I use bookies like bureaux de change, floating money across the counter from one currency to another, one whim to another, back and forth, till superstition reduces the differential to peanuts. It's pure madness but at least I know it.

If you've been to a bookies you'll see it's the only shop that has wastepaper baskets everywhere and virtually nothing else. Essentially, gamblers pay money to write words and numbers on pieces of paper, which are usually scrunched up and thrown into one of the bins. If an average race has ten runners, that's a ten percent chance per horse, as such. These aren't great odds.

The worst bit about a losing day is waking up and remembering how much it came to. If it's a four-figure sum I'm particularly morose and lay in bed thinking about when it might all end. I've not yet got to the stage when I actually decide how it may end, which will be when I know I'm in real trouble, but the thought does cross the mind when you lose big time.

I reenact the same thought process at the first moment of waking up after a gamble, which is most days.

The first thought is how much did I lose? I'll ponder this until I have a ballpark figure, which doesn't take long because it was probably my last thought before sleeping (especially if it was a particularly heavy loss).

Once the amount registers, a cold wave sweeps through me. To bat it off I resolve to check my balance on the bank app but that's not going to happen until much later in the day. I don't want to know. Then I'll wonder how much I have left on me in cash. At this time I'll grab my trousers by my bed and dive into the wallet for banknotes. I'll also look for betting slips to see if there are any unclaimed winners or bets still running.

With a cup of tea, I'll wonder how much I drank. Where was I? Did I get in any scrapes? Was I barred from anywhere? Is there any food in the flat? Did I text the lady? Do I have any pot to dull everything?

Chances are I was a shitshow so I chase through my mind to piece things together.

I live in a second floor flat at a housing association in Surrey. The flat next to me has a very bad record for suicide, the last two tenants killing themselves. The present tenant is a young guy I still haven't met. I don't think he comes out from the flat much but I know he's in there because the lights are always on and when I close the curtains before going to sleep his bedroom is lit by TV flickers. I should go and say hello but I just haven't bothered.

The guy who used to live in the flat below me was the biggest user of the emergency services for the entire county during 2019. I gave him a nickname, the six million dollar man.

For two years he drank from the moment he woke up to the moment he slept. He'd retired and gone back on the sauce after being left money by his mum.

The only reason he went out was to get more booze but he kept losing his keys and couldn't get back in. I must have had ten sets of keys cut for him. He was eventually sent to prison for a total of nineteen ASBOs, all for being drunk and disorderly outside the flat or in town.

On the day of his sentencing I was on my way downstairs going off to work when I saw two charity workers outside his flat door. They were there to help him get to court.

The door was ajar and these charity workers had a hand over their face. The stench in his flat is unbearably strong.

They told me he didn't want to go to court so I waded in with my t-shirt over my face.

They opened the door to bring better air in and I got him out of bed and into the bathroom to wash off the puke and shit with his showerhead, then patted him down with a towel and put him in his least soiled tracksuit. The charity workers wouldn't let him in their car so I drove him to the courthouse. We waited two hours before being led in like muppets.

There were three judges and they were all useless, just going through the motions like the police services, who, rather than actually helping, had only intervened to issue him with an ASBO time and again in the hope that he'd eventually top himself on the drink. The numerous charities that had tried to help were unable to when push came to shove.

Try as he might, he just wouldn't leave his mortal coil so he was sent down for ten weeks. He's in a care home now, thank God, but the flat's still empty. I think he's got a wet brain. It's a mean old world.

I thought about my losses in bed until about midday, then got up, made a cup of coffee and had a roll up in front of the box, then went to get a bottle of red, some food and roll ups from the supermarket before early Sunday closing at 4.30pm.

In the evening, I cried a few tears thinking about the children and did what I haven't done for quite some time; I looked for a Gamblers Anonymous meeting online and found that there was one every Tuesday at a church up the road.

Tired of television and moping around on the sofa, I decided to write down yesterday's shenanigans and I've been at it till now. I've totted up how much I'll need for the week's outgoings and it's tight but I'll just about do it. The one good thing about being on the breadline is that I can't afford to have a proper gamble so I don't really think about it. That's when I start to repair. Thankfully I didn't send that text to the lady. These are the small mercies of a feckless gambler.

I've just had a steak with potatoes and garlic mushrooms and it's almost time for bed so I've got away with it. The morose thoughts about the losses have almost evaporated and tomorrow's another day. It's imperative I think past the losses.

It's now the next day, Monday morning. I don't know what the bank holiday's for but there's hardly any traffic out. I'm glad I don't have to work.

What to do? I don't know. I haven't written a thing since before the lockdowns so it's probably time to give it another go.

*

It's a week later now.

I've been thinking of self-excluding again at the local bookies. It's just too easy to blow my load after a few beers. The last time I self-excluded was a shade over two years ago and it helped for a while. I'd blown an awful lot of money and gambling had taken me to my knees, again. I saved up a bit, but then the London bookies became a focus for when I saw the lady in town. The usual day would be to go for food and drinks somewhere, have a cuddle then take the bus back to Putney, where I parked, usually at about 5pm.

That's when I started using the bookies on Putney High Street. With a few extra pints on board, I'd usually lose a few hundred, sometimes win a hundred, the usual scraps. Soon after starting back up, I found a local bookies I'd overlooked in self-excluding and started going via there from time to time.

A few months ago, the two-year self-exclusion lapsed. It only took a little while to get me back to the bad old days, earning loads and gambling most of it away. Self-exclusion does seem the best way, but I know I won't do it. Not for now. I'm back on the merry go round and I don't want to get off. Or maybe I'm really on a Waltzer, spinning around so fast I can't get off. I'd break my neck.

I've got six thousand four hundred saved with the lady in her sock drawer and I don't want to touch that. Trouble is, I've started blowing all my earnings again, not saving a stitch, losing the lot.

During the last week, my love affair with fruit machines had been rekindled, a few flutters at a pub in Cranleigh on the premise of getting materials for the job I was doing down the road. With a decent DIY shop only a short walk from the pub I could park up, have a couple at the machine, get the stuff and then go back to work. The pubs were slowly starting to open up again and things looked a bit brighter. I've worked throughout lockdown, anything to get out of the flat. With the pubs closed for months at a time I found peace in painting on canvas at home at night with a few spliffs and a bottle of something.

I went to Haslemere on Saturday morning to see the new accountant. She's a lovely woman, an attractive single mum who lives with her little girl. She turned out to be a talker. The dad was long gone, an alcoholic who'd been difficult to remove from the house. She'd wanted a better life for her girl so he had to go.

After totting up my earnings against expenses, I owed the very manageable sum of eighty quid to the taxman, having paid a shade over two grand in income tax already by working for another painter.

I stopped at The Fox for a pint on the way back and then got the flavour to go back to the Cranleigh pub to gain revenge on the machine for a recent loss. I had a couple there and ended up losing about twenty quid. It filled a hole in my otherwise deathly dull as dishwater life.

Back home I watched the tail end of the racing and had a nap before my dull as dishwater evening got underway. The main thing was, I hadn't gone to the bookies.

If I haven't gambled on the Saturday I'm programmed to want a flutter on the Sunday. Until that thirst is satisfied, I'm just a gambler in waiting.

Sunday morning was much more morosely hideous than most and I woke up wanting no part in it. But then, the thought of gambling came into play so I cooked up some implausible plan to go to London and see an exhibition at Tate Britain. That's how gambling worms its way in, through some noble cause that seems perfectly reasonable but is actually just an excuse to get me down the bookies after a few pub visits.

I sat down and ate my boiled eggs with soldiers and tea and then looked up what was on at the Tate. I felt rough as hell. Breakfast did nothing to alleviate the trauma of living. At about ten I switched the telly on and realised I could easily watch it all day, anything to see through another boring Sunday without gambling.

The idea of going to an exhibition had been completely erased but London was still an option, and the new horizon I'd dreamt up now involved a pub in Soho for beers with intermittent flutters at my lucky bookies in Chinatown, just two minutes' walk from the pub. With lockdown over, I also wanted to sample some fruit machines, namely those at The Blue Posts next to the Ritz and the other place I can't remember the name of down a cul de sac off Jermyn Street. Having re-opened I was excited to see if they still had the old school machines. The new digital ones are taking over but they're as interactive as a rubber doll; money-washing machines that can rinse you in minutes. I needed to play an old one.

By about midday I'd parked up in Putney at my favourite spot (free on Sundays) and walked across the bridge to the tube. I got off at Earl's Court but didn't realise the Piccadilly Line was closed so I got back on the next one, then the loudspeaker said 'change for Piccadilly Line' so I stupidly got off again, then I got on the next one and got off at Victoria for the short change to Green Park.

I saw people outside The Posts so I waddled down there but the fruit machine had gone. I went to the other pub off Jermyn but their machine was gone too. Leaving with a huff, I understood that fruit machines weren't part of the new vision for pubs. I'd outgrown (or at least lived through) the explosive era of pub gaming machines, from Pacman and Space Invaders to the old Nudgematic machines and onto the now seemingly defunct one hundred pound jackpot machines.

At the Piccadilly end of Jermyn Street I saw two pigeons pecking at pavement puke. It was a honk of mess no doubt delivered the night before and as I stared at the pigeons pecking away happily I decided it must have been chips. There was nothing to it, just little bits of half digested white stuff. Then I imagined the puker; young, male, easily inebriated, hunched to make way for the expulsion of the unwanted load in order to resume his night out as if nothing had happened, perhaps giving it ten minutes to get back to the serious business of kissing his girl.

A liquid streak had made its way to the gutter. The offending alcohol was most probably lager, drunk far too quickly by a novice. A little pool had collected and dried out, leaving a residue at the gutter's edge.

I wanted to take a picture of the pigeons pecking away from a low angle to get in the gutter and the streak but they seemed to be enjoying themselves too much so I left them to it. That's a regret. I asked the pigeons if they knew what they were eating but they didn't even look up. The more central you go into London, the more brazen the pigeon.

The pub was heaving with the usual crowd so I got my pint in and downed it sharpish. With only one-twenty in the wallet and two-fifty in the bank I had to be prudent if I wanted to see the week out and avoid any awkward advances from customers. I took another swift one and then went over to the Chinatown bookies.

No one was wearing a mask when I got there but within a few minutes they'd all put them on and I wondered whether the presence of a lone Englishman had been the reason for their change of tack. Maybe they thought I was undercover old bill.

There was racing at Perth, York and somewhere else plus one in South Africa, one at Longchamp and two in Ireland. My first two bets came in, both virtuals at long odds, giving me winnings of about two hundred and fifty from my five pound each-way bets. I had some losers but a few each-way bets placed and I was holding my own very nicely. By the time I left I was still two-fifty up so I went back to the pub and sunk a pint outside. Everyone was talking animatedly and I realised I was the only person stood on his tod. An attractive woman kept staring at me as if she knew me or despised me or fancied me. I don't know which but it made me feel very uneasy. Every time I looked her way, there she was next to her man ogling me with fiercely intense eyes. It felt like she was eating me up in her mind, a real snake.

That was enough to move me on but I didn't want to go directly back to the bookies so I wandered up Dean Street and decided to try and find the pub where Jeffrey Bernard used to drink, as a sort of homage walkabout. I was sure it was off Soho Square but I couldn't find the place so I walked back towards the bookies, stumbling across the open air Soho Fest where someone was singing *New York, New York*. I wolfed down some veggie street food and hoped it wouldn't backfire with the beers on board.

Back at the bookies the large majority of gamblers had scarpered so there was much more room to move around and check the runners and riders on the newspapers dotted about the walls.

One virtual horse I remember the name of, Loveslayer, came in at 16/1. I'd only put two pound fifty each-way on her but she returned fifty odd so I thought I'd lump a ton on the nose of an odds-on favourite in a five-horse race at Perth. It came stone last but then I redeemed myself with a fiver each-way on a virtual nag that came in at 25/1, raising my overall winnings to three hundred and eighty quid. There'd been another very lucky win with a real race somewhere - in the flurry of placing the bet I'd forgotten to put it down as each-way so it returned almost double.

There's always some bookies shenanigans going on and this time it was to do with Longchamp, where the results were taking ages to come through. I had a measly each-way to come back from that and I knew I could easily lose a load waiting for payout with the beers wearing off. For some reason, though, I didn't let it bother me, remaining calm and kindly with the servers as I placed little bets on races. England were playing the mighty Andorra in a World Cup qualifier so I had a wacko bet on us beating them eleven-nil at 40/1.

Once the Longchamp result was announced I cashed in and

left, still three-eighty up. I took another beer at the pub and then walked down to Piccadilly for the number fourteen bus. It was packed. Hot and sticky by the time I got to Fulham I was in dire need of another pint so I stopped in at The Eight Bells.

Greed is the sworn enemy of reason for any gambler. It can make mincemeat of any winnings in no time, but even as I supped at my lager I was already thinking of going for a lucky last at The Racket over the bridge. They'd surely still have the old school fruities.

I drained my pint and walked at a brisk pace over the bridge but guess what? All three had been replaced with the new digital ones. I got a pint in and saw a gambler sat at one. He had a red, angry loser's face but I couldn't resist using the one next to him. I broke even on a twenty and thought I was being cautious when I went out for a roll up but once I sat down all I could think of was waiting for the loser to leave so I could swoop down and grab the winnings off his machine.

He'd gone when I went back in for another pint so I started playing his. Twenty minutes later two hundred quid had gone straight through the thing. I got to thinking that he'd played me, throwing the old loser card in to see how greedy I was. We're all rats, gamblers are. Or maybe I'm just paranoid.

I was out of twenties so I shoved a fifty in but it spat it out. Asking a barmaid to change it up, she said it was company policy not to take fifties because of a recent spate of fakes so I finished my pint off fuming and marched up Putney High Street, knowing what I had to do. Pints installed, it was time to win big or lose the lot.

Betfred was empty apart from the old boy with dementia on his machine. He'll always be there around teatime, constantly asking the servers which button to press. Heartbreaking but what can you do?

I was in there for at most an hour and must have placed about twenty-five bets in all. Every single one was a loser. I'd spent the five hundred in cash and rinsed the account of two hundred, leaving fifty in there for the week's food and roll up expenditure. With half a tank of fuel I'd be fine getting to work. I had a few bills going out on Wednesday and would see the dental hygienist on Friday but as long as I got loads done by midweek I'd be sweet for an advance.

Searching in my pockets for loose change I did a one-pound forecast on a virtual and the server gave me that look of bewildered pity as he slid the slip over to me.

Walking out onto the street, electricity was fizzing around my body, emotions struggling to keep up with the fury my brain was trying to process. If someone had bumped into me they'd have got a big shock.

Stopping for a full minute outside The Spotted Horse, knowing a pint would settle my nerves for the drive home, I went in. It was a terrible pint and I struggled to wrap my chops around the glass, liquid falling from my mouth and down to my chin as if I'd just come out from a jab at the dentist's. I didn't even have the strength to wipe if off so it just dripped into my lap as I counted the costs of the day. In all I was about three-fifty down, having wiped clean almost four hundred quid of pure profit in an hour and a half.

I stopped outside Tesco but was too ashamed to go in and get some cream and milk for my carbonara and tea in the morning. The drive back was horrible. I kept thinking about something I'd seen on one of those traffic cop programs.

In it, an obliterated drunk driver had ploughed into the back of a car at a roundabout. He was too pissed to talk on camera and couldn't remember what happened, or so he reckoned. The traffic cop described him as like all drunk drivers, 'too selfish to think about anyone else but themselves.' I knew he was right. In the end the driver was heavily fined and had his licence taken away for three years.

When I got home I started worrying that I'd spent everything from my account and began composing a text to the lady to ask for some money to tide me over. The text read something like this; 'Sorry to break our silence but could you put a hundred into my account please? If you go to my bank with cash it won't show up on your side'.

That was the last thing I wanted to do. We've been sworn to a break for a while now, so she could sort things out her end (it's complicated). Me asking this would undoubtedly leave her thinking the worst, that I'd never change, which is probably true. The worst feeling is that I'll lose her for good. I can't handle the thought of that but it's probably only right and correct to let her get on with her life. It just wouldn't work if we got together and I'm pretty sure we both think so. There's not much we can do about it.

Sleep was awful. I kept waking up with a headache, knowing that if I took some pain relief I might have to throw up. Little advertising jingles raced through my mind, then the composition of the as yet unsent text kept rattling on. At dawn I resolved not to go to work. I needed to write this down. Maybe it could help me stop gambling. Or something. Anything.

I wanted to check my account to see how much was left but fear stopped me. Apart from the two hundred I knew I'd spent on the card I was sure I'd placed a few small bets on top at the end, which would leave me with peanuts. The Spotted Horse was on the card too.

At nine I got up to call the customer and say I wasn't feeling a hundred percent. I'm way up high on a large set of ladders this week so I need to be on the ball. He was fine about it so I said I'd see him the next day at nine. If I get a big day in on Tuesday I'm sure he'll advance me the necessary readies to settle my bills.

I went back to bed and slept well for a bit, then got up and checked the account. There was still about fifty quid left so I went to the supermarket and got some food. Home again I made a fry up and felt vaguely human at about two in the afternoon. At four I went to see an old customer about a job she needed doing. She'd written in a text that she wanted it done next spring so I thought I'd go and give her a price to firm it up anyway.

We went around the house and I gave my price, to which she agreed, asking if I could do it immediately. It's autumn but the forecast's fine for the next two weeks.

So I was back in the game, a six grand job only a few minutes' walk from home! But what in hell good was money ever going to be if I just burned it at the bookies as soon as it appeared in my account? Such are the pathetic quandaries of a ridiculous gambler with a drink problem.

*

It's now the following Sunday. I did it again yesterday.

On Friday, in an attempt to stave off a weekend gambling session, I texted the lady I'm starting work with on Monday to see if I could bring it forward to a Saturday start. She replied that wasn't convenient but would transfer a three hundred quid advance for materials. So I had that plus a few quid in the wallet.

As always I wasn't fully aware that I'd gamble. Actually, come to think of it, after getting the transfer on Friday night, I searched online to see who was playing in the Saturday football and had quietly resigned myself to a cheeky accumulator, which meant going to the bookies.

I self-excluded from all online UK gambling sites about four years ago after losing a grand in an hour on Christmas morning. About a week or two after I did that, I kept getting emails from Yahoo telling me that I needed to update my app otherwise I'd risk losing all my history. When I updated it, I found that the only difference was that I now had adverts on the homepage, directly above the latest incoming email.

These ads were almost entirely from gambling firms, offering free bets for joining their sites. I tried to get in touch with Yahoo but they didn't reply so now, every time I go to email, I'm bombarded with ads from Sky and Virgin and all the other shysters. Then there's all the ads on the telly, the sponsorship on footy teams' shirts, the hoardings around stadia, the pubs. It's everywhere. They're like stalkers on a common.

Waking up on Saturday I had my poached egg on toast, washed the car and finally lugged up one of the boxes of artwork that failed to sell at Portobello a few months back. They'd been sat disconsolately on the backseat.

I looked again at the teams playing. It was about eleven by then so I cooked up an innocent enough plan.

Heading out to the car at half eleven I had an hour till the early kick off so I went to the decorating centre and got some basic materials for the job, namely a tub of masonry paint, a tin of undercoat (oil-based of course, the water-based stuff is like most modern reinventions; a poor alternative to its predecessor) and some two-part wood filler for the timbers.

Even when I'm a complete tool of a gambler, I'm still the most honest house painter out there. I take pride in my work and because it takes five years to see its enduring quality, customers take that long to trust me, at which time I'm quite happily put on another job with them. I only use the right materials and never cut corners, in stark contrast to my private life, which as you know is littered with poor decision-making and shoddy behaviour. I suppose my work ethic is the real me and my conduct elsewhere is the poisoned me. Or maybe I'm just a slave to work in order to feed my gambling.

After the decorating centre, which relieved me of seventy-five quid, I drove to the bookies up the road and asked about how to do an accumulator on one of the new machines.

The lady showed me to a fixed odds betting terminal, as they're called. It was really easy to use so I put a tenner bet on a six-way accumulator.

On this occasion, I'd made a pact with myself to only have a couple of bets on horses to the value of a tenner in total so I went over to the screens and looked for names. There was a virtual horse called Agnes at 12/1 so I quickly scribbled my bet down, two pound fifty each-way. I chose Agnes because that was the name of the psychotherapist I'd seen for about six months up until about three years ago. I'd see her every Saturday morning and for the first few months I kept off the gambling, but then I let things slide.

By coincidence, I'd bumped into her just the day before on the way to getting my bread from the market. The funny thing is I farted audibly as I clocked eyes on her and then remembered the session when she must have farted just prior to my arrival, both of us trying to act as if we couldn't smell it.

Agnes came in and paid out forty-two quid fifty so I placed another bet on a South African race. There was a bloke singing his own praises to the lady behind the till. He was talking about his two kids and how his mum and his aunt always said how he'd be a great dad because he was such a lovely lad, how he did everything for his kids because they needed proper nurturing, which he'd provide. I wondered what his job was, definitely the building trade but I couldn't put a finger on it. During the race his horrible voice drowned out the commentary and I almost asked him to pipe down but I didn't want to ruin my buzz. My nag came nowhere and moments later his dog came in.

Striding up to the till he passed his slip over and said, loudly, 'that should be two hundred and forty back'. I totted it up; a 5/1 winner paying two-forty meant he'd staked forty quid and won two hundred. Lucky lad.

Counting out his money, twice, he came back over to the screens beaming. He tried to make conversation but I just nodded, then he announced that he'd be off. I imagined him getting a skinful at the pub then returning home to play nasty little mind games with his wife and kids.

The next virtual race, I placed a couple of two pound fifty each-way bets on a pair of nags. One of them came in at 10/1 so I picked up my winnings and left, the eighty quid in my wallet swollen to a heady one-twenty with my accumulator paid for.

I knew what I'd do next and went to a country pub that I like. There was a heaving crowd of very loud people, a wedding posse fresh from the day before. This was their hangover lunch and judging by the crap that came out of their gobs they'd already had a skinful.

I sat as far away as I could in the large lawned garden. After a couple of swift ones I could take no more and the urge to bet was on me. I stopped off at another pub for one more pint and then passed by a pair of charity shops to see if they had any DVDs. I found *Taxi Driver* in unused condition for a quid. The previous day I'd found *Kind Hearts and Coronets* at an Oxfam plus an old book called *The Loneliness of The Long Distance Runner*, which I read a portion of feverishly that morning.

With the inevitable upon me I got back in the car and drove around the corner to park outside the bookies. This being my least lucky bookies in the entire world meant that it wouldn't be too hard to reconcile if I lost my load.

It was about three in the afternoon and a full card of racing was well underway. There were two blokes there, both with northern accents. We did our thing quite happily together. Reasonably well oiled I was in the groove and placed twenty each-way on some nag at Navan, which came stone last. One of the chaps whooped when the winner crossed the line but he didn't rub our noses in it like the twat at the last place.

In the next race a horse called Wiff Waff streaked past the leaders right at the death and snatched victory on the line by a whisker. As soon as the commentator mentioned his name, 'and who's this on the outside? It's Wiff Waff!' I burst out laughing.

Wiff Waff had sailed in at 8/1 and if I hadn't been conjuring up a winner on a virtual race I'd have definitely lumped large on him. What a name! But I hadn't, so it was time to start throwing money about.

With half-time looming in the football, none of my teams in the accumulator were winning. They weren't losing either, just drawing, so I was still in the game. On entering the bookies I'd placed forty on a Wolves win at about evens and they were drawing too. They'd lost one-nil in their last three games to really good teams so I knew they were ripe for reward.

In the next race there was a horse called Oh So Squelchy, bouncing about at 8/1, so I went twenty each-way on him. One of the other chaps, who had the look of a man on a long losing streak at home, work and the bookies, decided to saddle his interest in Oh So Squelchy, putting down a similar bet. The thing came nowhere.

I saw him looking towards the door as if it was a portal to another planet or at least a way out from this hell. I knew just how he felt. After a few more losers he picked himself up from his stool and just stood there.

'Go on,' I said, 'you can do it.'

He took it the right way but he was still glued to the spot.

'That's me done,' he said finally, with that stupefied sniff of tired resolution.

'Best move you've made all day, mate. See ya.'

He dragged up a laugh as he opened the door and walked out.

I'd already blown what was in the wallet and felt the flavour for another pint so I raced off to some crap hole, necked it and returned with gusto, knowing the card would need to be used. Well into the second half of the football, two of my six teams in the accumulator were one up, which bode quite well considering I was in the worst bookies in the world. My ten-pound stake would only net me a hundred and twenty but I'd started to look upon it as my saving grace for the week ahead. Wolves were still drawing so there was hope there too.

An old favourite called Vandad was in the next race and I started to think about the significance of his name alongside my present circumstances. For the last two months I've been itching to leave the flat, buy an old van and go off grid. Van dad; a dad, who hasn't seen his daughters for twelve years, living in a van in pub car parks.

The lady has my savings stashed in her sock drawer but I don't want to ask for any, as you know. With winter looming it's bad timing but I absolutely detest where I live and I'm in no position to make plans finding a new place unless by some miracle I can find a swap with another resident in social housing. I've wanted to move back to London for a year now but there's been no luck on the swapping site so far. I've had a few bites but no takers so the idea of getting out of social housing altogether and buying a van has become quite interesting. I've always been a nomad anyway.

I can't rent privately because I'd never tick all the boxes for the estate agents and landlords, what with all the hoops you have to jump through, even for a crappy studio above a tanning shop. It's harder to rent than it is to get a mortgage but I don't have enough for a deposit so that's out. Plus I'm not young any more and I don't have a guarantor. I can't even think about renting a room in a shared house. That would tip me over the edge.

Vandad was one of five horses so I used the card to put forty each-way on him. At 3/1 I'd almost get my money back if he came second and if he won I could clear off and count my lucky stars.

Rounding the last turn home two of the nags had dropped out, one falling very badly.

There in the straight, one or two furlongs out, Vandad was holding his own with the other two. Now it was a question of who pushed the button first and it was Vandad, the jockey giving him the whip with force. He didn't really respond, though, and the other two found more. The whip came out on all three of them but the reserves of each seemed similarly spent. As one of the other jockeys was smashing the crap out of his horse from his right hand, Vandad switched to the inside and drew closer.

I could see that the other chap had sided with Vandad because he was involuntarily moving forward in his chair towards the screen, something gamblers do without being conscious of it. He was almost up and over the screwed-in table as Vandad crossed the line a neck behind the other two bastard nags.

The commentator later reported that the horse that fell would have to be put down, another victim of the slave trade.

I placed sixty quid on a dog, which lost by a nose. It was time to go to the pub to look at the full-time results on the phone and nurse a pint so I sped off in the car. Sat in the garden it was more like a fucking crèche with truckloads of kids tearing around the place. Those young parents gave me that look they give middle-aged men on their own so I smiled back sardonically as if to say 'yes, I'm here to ogle your prize possessions, you fat old bag of shite'.

My Wolves bet was a winner and four of my six teams in the accumulator had won, leaving the late kick-off and another match the next day to complete the win. I drained my pint and went back to collect on Wolves but he'd shut up shop. Being an out of town bookies they close early and I'd forgotten. I knocked on the door and waved my ticket but he mouthed sorry so I got back in the car and drove off to a pub on the way home. I had just enough for a pint with the remaining pocket shrapnel so I drained one and then left, neither here nor there in my head.

I'd lost two-fifty on the day but Wolves would return eighty and the accumulator was still on. The late kick-off had won so there was another potential one-twenty there, which meant I'd only be fifty down on the weekend's madness if it came in.

At just past two in the afternoon the next day I went to the bookies to collect on Wolves. When the lady showed me how to use the terminal the day before she told me there was a cash-out option on the accumulator so I decided to have a look and see what it would pay without waiting for the last match to go ahead. If the cash-out was more than sixty quid I'd take it because I had a funny feeling I'd get bitten on the arse if I kept it going.

She showed me how to find out on the machine and it was fifty-five quid. I asked her what she'd do but she gave nothing away.

Time was on my side. An hour before a Premier League match, the team selections are revealed online so I decided to wait till then to make my mind up. I cashed the Wolves bet in and got eighty-four quid so I went to the screens and immediately won a virtual race at 12/1. A few bets later I was back down to eighty odd but then another virtual came in. I started talking to an old boy and we just chewed the fat for a while as I placed a pound each-way bets on throwaway virtuals. Like me, he generally had much better luck on the virtuals than the real races. I told him I'd given up on form and just went with the horse's name, the funnier the better, virtual or not. He did much the same and I could tell he meant it because he went through his process of elimination, based entirely on the name of his daughter and his grandma, Anna and Granna. If a name popped up with something close to either he'd give it a go. I asked if he'd put anything on Vandad the day before but that fell on deaf ears.

I kept the bet riding and the match started. I needed Liverpool to win and they were set for an easy away victory at Leeds. There was a bloke singing the praises of Leeds and swearing a lot. The lady behind the till told me she was actually a Liverpool fan and that I was onto a winner but I just grimaced. My bets weren't going well and I was down to forty quid. I knew that if Liverpool lost I'd have pretty much nothing to live on for the week so I curbed my little bets and started thinking about the pub. Then Liverpool scored so I put a cheeky bet on a virtual and it came in. I'd written it down as an each-way but she paid me out on the nose, forty-two quid instead of late twenties. At half-time and still one up I went for a pint, the one in the country from yesterday.

When I got to the bar I waited for a while and then one of the barmen told me it was a private party. He was sorry but I couldn't be served. I got to thinking they'd had enough of me, the loner guy who asked for no froth, so I went to the pub I use after work most days, which was on my way home anyway.

They'd had a big Sunday lunch session but being almost six it had tapered off and they were joking around behind the bar so I got my pint and sat outside. I checked the score and Liverpool had gone two up. With only five minutes left the bet was as good as safe so I started reading some of my old stuff on a website I used to play around on, back in the days when I was still sure I'd get published.

A little boy of about two came up to where I was sitting and just stood there staring at me. His dad had been following him around the garden as if he was about to step on a mine and I could see his mum staring at me to find out if I was trying to indulge her little lad's gaze.

It's hard not to at least smile when a little life form looks at you with such stern curiosity so I grimaced at him with one of my little half smiles but that only made him come a step closer. The dad was well on guard by then, hovering behind the boy with arms out like a ghost.

'Come on, Tommy. Where's Mummy? Come on, Tom.' He was talking to him as if he was a dog. Kneeling next to him with his hands out to guide him elsewhere, the little thing shook his head defiantly. He wouldn't budge.

I felt too awkward to return his gaze so I picked up the phone as a form of distraction, which was the dad's prompt to scoop the lad up and take him away. It's turned into such a shitty world.

With the win in the bag I had a second pint and then went

home. The lady I'm working for texted to say she was going in for an operation, that she'd have to self-isolate afterwards but not to take it the wrong way. I texted back to say all was fine and that I'd see her tomorrow.

I watched *Taxi Driver* and blubbered like a baby at the end when Travis shoots the pimps and saves the day. Tonight I'll watch *Kind Hearts and Coronets* and probably laugh my socks off. The oldies are still the best. I forgot to say that I bought my first new book from an actual bookshop for about five years on Friday. It's called *The Heart of a Dog* by one of my favourite satirists, Bulgakov. I read it in one sitting on Friday afternoon. Here's to a good week's work.

*

I tore into the job on Monday morning, chisel hammering, gouging and tungsten-scraping rot at a large bay window. By midday I'd collected two buckets of dead rotten wood, old putties and cracked cement. For lack of rain over the last fortnight the rot was generally dry as a bone. I let the sun have its way with the inner dampness for a couple of hours, then in the afternoon, ready to fill, I asked the lady of the house if there were any stones around the garden and if so could I have a few.

Her husband took me to the end of the garden, where there were some lovely large pebbles in a pond. He said I could take some from there so we threw a dozen or so into a bucket, then we sifted the flowerbeds and found some good, angular flint pieces. Back at house I cleaned the stones off on the grass and let them dry out on the patio. Placing a few of the bulbous pebbles into the vertical to horizontal joint of the heavily gouged oak sill, they looked the part.

No one had done a decent job of that bay window for over

half a century. The rot probably started setting in about then and, during that time, with botched measures eked out by the various painters of the past, the sills and joints had finally deteriorated to such an appalling state that they needed the true love.

I'd gouged two eighteen inch wide holes that went right back to brick and window. If a chippy was brought in at this point, he'd have to chop out and replace most of the sill with properly seasoned oak, which is like gold dust. He'd be a good two grand in all, but even then I'd have to fill and shape his joints. By doing it myself, I was saving the customer about £1700 and me the aggro of getting a decent chippy in.

With the largest pebbles placed into the joints, I knocked up and smacked in a fistful of epoxy resin, a two-part filler similar to car filler that dries hard as a golf ball in minutes. Save getting a chippy in, this is the only real remedy to the age-old problem of rot. It's just as good a bond as today's oak, stone and epoxy resin lashed together.

Imagine massive holes at joints eaten away by decades of rampant termite and lice abuse. Think of Parliament, a house of cards, empty on the inside.

After the primary fill around and into the laid stones I have a trick of applying the next batch of filler and then, while it's drying, sticking a nice lengthy piece in there to shape up angles for further filling. Flint's good for that because it's angular and edgy. At twenty quid a kilo the filler's not cheap so I can save a lot this way. Some say that the weight of the stones corrupts the integrity of the bond but I put in copious amounts of wood filler to make the hold genuine. I've got loads of tricks like that.

At six in the evening, drained but satisfied, I was done for the day. With rent on Wednesday I was about to broach the question of a small advance when the lady of the house announced that she'd be going into hospital again on Wednesday. A thousand had been put into my account. She and her husband remarked on the thoroughness of the work and it felt good in my veins and heart.

Honestly, though, the first thing I thought when she said she'd dumped a grand into the account was how I'd cope without gambling the following day, Tuesday, knowing it was a washout. I said I'd go in if the forecast cleared up but it looked decidedly soggy all day long.

With the rent going out on Wednesday I'd have five hundred extra sloshing about. But what if I had a real blowout and lost the lot? I've lost so many flats and house shares like that but I've been good in this housing association place. I've paid without fail every month for six years, even if it meant bringing in a favour during winter or after a particularly bad run of luck. Thing is, at five hundred a month I don't feel like I'm getting ripped off. If this place was private it would be double and treble that with no security. They could sell the place any time or just hike the price up out of reach to get me gone for a flip.

Tuesday morning I got up and made tea, looked out the window. Sodden wet ground and a thick drizzle with big pregnant clouds everywhere. A definite washout.

I took a call from a woman in Wonersh Park, a classy enclave of million pound plus houses where I've done loads of work, so I went over and saw that at about eleven. I couldn't give her a price because she was having walls taken down and new plaster everywhere but we had a good chinwag.

Back in the car I started getting the flavour but it wasn't even midday so I called a customer I'd worked for the previous week and asked if I could pop round to wipe down some mildew from a large external ceiling that I'd eggshelled the previous year. I wanted to keep it nice for them and they'd given me a tip so it was about right. They were heading off to the airport for a holiday so that was out.

Driving back to town I'd made up my mind to go to the pub but I couldn't decide which one. Then I thought about The

Willy in the country but when I got there it was closed. Sat in the car with money to burn I decided to go to Dorking and pretend to be Drew Pritchard in the antique shops. I could park slightly outside town and get a few leisurely pints in between my shrewd vintage purchases, or so I thought.

When I got to its outskirts there were residents' parking signs everywhere and no free spots anywhere. Those days seem to have gone for good now.

I went to a car park just down West Street and paid for two hours at a pound a pop, not too bad. I did go to one or two antique shops but they were dire so I strolled up the high street and went around the charity shops. I've been looking for books by a guy called Celine because Bukowski keeps banging on about how he's his favourite ever writer but you just can't find them any more. I asked the manager at the Oxfam bookshop where the decent pubs were and he told me a lot of them had closed down and turned into coffee shops etc.

Honestly, I'd never been to Dorking before but it spooked me out. It felt like the most detached place on earth, zapping my energy so much I had to have a flutter at Coral, where I should have sided with the Racing Post's nap at the first race at Fontwell but went with Snug As A Bud instead, a 2/1 favourite I'd seen win the week before. Obviously the nap came in so I went to a pub near the car park and had a pint of Hells and a go on the fruit machine. It was an old school machine, a Spartacash. I won about four quid, necked the pint and got the hell out of Dorking.

On the way back I stopped off for a pint somewhere and the food smelt great. I saw a woman eating fish and chips but I couldn't resign myself to pay the seventeen quid. There was a ten-pound portion and when I asked about that the barmaid pointed to a sticklike old boy picking with a juddering hand at a measly side plate. I necked a pint of Peroni with a fag outside and skidded off up the road to Shere.

The one at the top there used to be a spit and sawdust pub but now it's another posh eatery with the grey paint, open fire and knocked down walls. There were some yummy mummies doing lunch.

Again I wanted to get something down me but the lamb was twenty-one quid so I sat outside under a parasol with my pint and smoked a few fags in the spitting rain, knowingly relishing the thought of my next port of call.

There's a back road to Cranleigh from Shere, up over the Surrey Hills, so I got in the car and weaved my way over to play the fruit machine at The Three Horseshoes. Trouble was, it was shut. A Tuesday. I couldn't work it out.

Not only had I self-excluded from the bookies in Cranleigh about two years ago after losing a shedload, I'd also told the manageress of the pub opposite to do one with the shitty Peroni pipes that stunk the pint out. In hindsight, it may have been her barrels.

But pride would have to take a backseat this time. The urge was too great and I needed to satisfy my craving so I sped over there and parked up on a one-hour spot.

The pub was shut. There was a sign saying they were now closed on Mondays and Tuesdays.

I waddled over the road and pushed at the door of the bookies. I'd gambled on there being a new manager and I was right. He didn't recognise me so I placed a quick bet on a virtual race to get the monkey off my back. It came stone last so I started looking at the screens for another race.

There were the usual two old boys there and one other thickset guy who kept on losing and going out to the cashpoint, conveniently positioned next door. He must have lost a good grand in the half hour I was there.

Me? I lost about a hundred quid in the end. I lost on every single virtual horse race but won on two virtual dogs at good odds and two real nags, all on the nose. Every single one of my each-way bets came nowhere and I thanked my lucky stars when I totted up that I must have wagered about a grand and only lost a paltry ton. This was a win. The rent was intact and I had well enough for the week. If I ploughed on at the job I reckoned I could have a decent weekend without calling in any advances, which would have been impossible anyway because the lady of the house is in hospital till Monday getting over the op.

I'd parked outside the fish and chip shop and the smell was too good to pass over so I got a small cod and chips (six pound seventy thank you very much). Back in the car I got on the road and started picking at the chips on the passenger seat as I drove, trying to work out where I should park to eat. In the end I plumped on outside the village stores in Shamley Green.

By this time I was in idiot mode with my little wooden fork stabbing at the lovely cod. A woman in an SUV decided to park in between two cars, blocking the road out. She sauntered into the shop, leaving hardly any room for the passenger of one of the adjacent cars to get out. As a guy wrestled with his door I shouted for him to tell the woman she's an idiot when he sees her inside. He nodded with a cautious smile.

By the time I'd finished my fish and chips she still hadn't come back so I beeped my horn for about ten seconds. The poor driver of the adjacent car, whose passenger was probably stuck in the queue behind the bitch, screeched off. I was so enraged by her audacity I wanted to go in there and give her a piece of my mind but you can't be too careful when you've got a few on board.

Next stop was a little pub on the way home for a pint of Peroni. The headache had already started up so I sunk it quick and left to watch about four episodes of the second series of *Nighty Night*, my only investment of all the charity shops in strange old Dorking. At about eleven I turned in without taking any pain relief, glugging down a half pint of water for good measure.

Sleep wasn't great but I had another good day's work on Wednesday. It turned out the conservatory's woodwork's in an even worse state than the bay window. Installed about twenty years ago the 'hardwood' for the lengthy sills was all but shot.

I hacked, chiselled and chivvied out the dry and wet rot. At certain areas, it had reached the internal brickwork.

Someone had squirted tubes of silicone all along and into what must have been a gaping crack between the sill and the upright, causing the wood to slowly rot undetected over time. Silicone and wood don't get along. Silicone weeps, causing damp.

By four I was knackered and sweating profusely from the sun on my back. The tiresome but ultimately rewarding work had got the better of me.

I like delving deep into the rot and taking it out for good, like a dentist, drilling to the core of the matter and filling it with the good stuff. I'd be back to the pond in the morning, fishing out some more prize pebbles and taking nicely angled flint from the flowerbeds for the more tricky areas. With the epoxy resin and its bond with the stones I'd put that sill to bed for good.

The man of the house had enquired at the hospital as to his wife's progress but after three or four calls all he'd been told was that she was out of theatre. To take his mind off things he'd gone for various walks and in the afternoon he'd treated himself to an online auction but the painting he wanted, by a lesser known Royal Academian, sold at way over the estimate and he had to let it go.

It's Saturday morning just after seven-thirty. Hacking out and filling the conservatory's woodwork has taken the whole week but it's pretty much there now. My back started playing up on Wednesday but the nerve that usually goes didn't quite budge enough to put me out of the game. It's been standing on the muscle but crucially it hasn't tangled up under my shoulder wing, which means I don't have to see the osteopath and take pain relief for the following two days, after which it's right as rain again. Rather than let it win it's best to keep on working. It tends to trick the old body into thinking I'm winning, or maybe it's just happy for the exercise. Either way, lolling about at home waiting for it to clear up only makes it worse.

I've been trying to cash in a miniscule pension for about a month now. Two or three weeks ago, after waiting the obligatory half-hour on the phone, I was told that a form would be sent out for me to sign and return. This could take up to two weeks to arrive, she said. Once that was received and sent back it would take five working days to process, at which time my final pension pot would be calculated. Then it would take up to eight weeks to receive the cheque.

I waited the two weeks for the form but it didn't arrive so I called from work and did a bit of filling while I waited for someone to answer. I told her what had happened and she said she'd send the form out by special delivery. I'd get it the next day guaranteed. It came but there was no form inside, just the usual crap about the alternatives I could choose from when deciding on what to do with my pension. The next day I called again and waited the thirty minutes, explaining the situation. This one presented the first barefaced lie.

During my first conversation there was a ten-minute process to trigger the release of my pension. I was asked again and again what I was choosing to do ('take the whole pot') but apparently at the end of the process I'd said I wanted to 'consider my options', which meant I wasn't fully sure. She said the form couldn't have been sent (the previous one said it had already been sent, but strangely never arrived) as I hadn't consented to release my pension. Rather than get her back up I gently requested that the form be sent so I can withdraw my pension pot. This will now take up to two weeks.

The reason I'm taking it out is because a barman told me there's going to be a massive stock market crash around November, which is fast approaching. This morning, flicking through news items online, I saw a piece on state pensions being delayed. People who'd paid in for forty-five years weren't able to take out their pensions from the government. There was no getting around the backlog in processing. The Department of Work and Pensions likes having our money far too much to give it back.

I don't know what's tougher, earning it or trying to keep it. Banks and governments serve themselves first, then each other, then they do everything in their power to restrict freedoms. What a bunch of termites, eating away at integrity like rot at a window sill.

Rather than let the bastards take my peace of mind I ended the conversation with the psychopath clerk and thanked her for her time. That's the way to deal with these termites because they enjoy nothing more than making your life more miserable than it already is.

With the sun beating down all day I was worn out from the filling by about two-thirty. If it hadn't been for the pebbles and flint I'd have used another ten kilos of filler. The main thing was the job would last. I could guarantee that because it would still be in one piece even if a bomb dropped on the house. The conservatory would be gone but there, glued to the top bricks and the old wood, my filler would hold firm those stones. Well, maybe.

Three of the lower plinths, actually made from softwood, had blown completely. It would take another five kilo tub of filler and a day to build up and shape it into the form of the plinths so the man of the house agreed that I should build up a basic angle for water to drain away and leave it at that. They hardly ever opened the windows and it wouldn't show the basic finish so no one would be the wiser.

I felt the flavour for a pint so I drove off to a country pub and had two there. I couldn't resist looking at the racing online and before I knew it I was back in the car, heading off to my least lucky bookies. On the way I had a pint at a crap hole where I've lost tens of thousands on the fruit machine over the years.

When I walked in I saw that they'd finally succumbed to the corporate plan and replaced the old school fruit machines with the crappy new digital ones.

I got my pint and in twenty minutes I was seventy quid down but then it gave me some free spins and I clawed back about forty-five quid so I drained the pint and went to the bookies.

There was one other guy there, an old boy busy spending his pension in the best way he knew. What else could he do? Join the church and listen to people squabbling about phone masts and parking restrictions? Why be politically correct when the political are corrupt?

I've now waited over a month for news on my kids. Their mum loves nothing more than to hold me captive to her powers of alienation.

I had about eighty quid in the wallet and the rent had gone out so there was only a shade under three hundred in the account, not that I wanted to use any of that because I knew I might be seeing the lady at the weekend.

There was a five-horse race at Yarmouth so I put a tenner each-way on an outsider but it came nowhere, then I saw a brilliantly named horse running at the next race at Vaal in South Africa. The horse's name was Daddy Time, a wacky outsider at 33/1 in a twelve-horse maiden.

Drawing a slip from its perch at the wall I put a tenner each-way on Daddy Time, then I saw another outsider and decided to hedge my bets by doing a five-pound each-way on both instead.

There was no commentary to the race so it was hard to tell who was where but as they turned into the straight and brought out the whips I could see that Daddy Time, number eleven, was in the lead, closely pursued by one other horse. I closed my eyes and tried to conjure up the images of my two girls but those days are well gone now so I just mumbled a short prayer under my breath.

All but Daddy Time were having the shit whipped out of

them without response so I knew I was in with a shout. Daddy Time found more and drew clear but then the other horse gained momentum under a good ride and regained a few lengths to come lashing back into contention. They flashed past the line together but I knew my boy had won. At a fiver each-way I picked up about two hundred quid.

Approaching closing time there was one final race. A Johnston horse running with Norton on board, 9/1, with two firm favourites at about 2/1 each. It was a seven-horse race and all the others were at least 7/1. By and large, in a race like this, all the money goes on the two favourites. That's the way the primitive mind or the novice gambler works, much like voting in politics. Equally likely is that the two firm favourites do no good.

Johnston knows how to ready a horse and has a good record at Ayr so I put a fiver each-way on Enfranchised, my 9/1 shot.

It was a one mile six furlong affair and as they approached three out I could see Enfranchised holding his own in fifth place. Ahead of him two horses were getting the whip but the other two were cruising.

Franny drew the whip out but didn't use it at first, preferring to nudge his arms' strength into the neck of the nag to ask for a response. The two flagging horses dropped away and one of the more comfortable ones was beginning to flag. It turned out that the other leading horse was one of the favourites but when Enfranchised passed him without trouble I knew he'd win. The favourite was whipped to shit for about five seconds but then the jockey gave up.

Enfranchised came first, followed by a 12/1 outsider who'd overtaken the favourite at the death, leaving the each-way favourite backers at a state of total loss and out of the frame. Nothing new there.

I left with three hundred quid in the wallet so a country pub was in order to sink a couple more before going home. That was Thursday.

On Friday I spoke with the lady in the morning. It was the first time for a week that we'd spoken and the line was terrible. Usually it's me that gets worked up but this time she was the one swearing, which I found quite endearing. Because of the very delicate situation we're in I'm giving her all the time she needs without any expectation on my part. She said that if things panned out right we could meet on Saturday night for supper and a few drinks in Soho.

I worked my tits off till four so I went for a couple in town (six quid a pint!) and then walked back home.

It's Saturday morning. There's no way I'm betting and drinking if I'm meeting the lady later so it looks like a very easy day. I might go to the dump with a load of my unsold children's books. They've been lying around the flat gathering dust. It's nine-thirty now so I'll go into town and see what's what in the charity shops. The flat needs a tidy too. I wanted to do a few hours' work but the lady of the house is returning from hospital so I should give her some space. Maybe I'll do a cheeky accumulator on the football, I don't know, but I can't wait to see the lady. She's a lot of fun. You'd love her.

*

It's about a month on now and I've gambled throughout. The lady and I have entered another period of silence so that she can focus on matters at home.

It's been almost three weeks since we last spoke and I'm struggling. I want to text her brother to ask if I can speak to her and find out how she is. I know I mustn't.

My gambling and drinking have escalated to the point where I really don't care whether I win or lose. My compulsion is constantly fed by alcohol, loneliness, shame and a very dark view of the future.

I'm in my own little process, though, having found someone to mutually exchange my flat with. He lives in Brixton and that's where I hope to be by Christmas. The authorities aren't exactly playing ball but we're on course. The main thing is that he's as set on moving as I am, but you never know. He may change his mind and stay put. I've had it with Guildford, even if it means I have to commute back for work.

I've been very busy on the work front for the last month, two outdoor jobs at lovely houses with good people. The weather has held up remarkably well for the time of year. It's November on Monday and I'll complete the second of the two jobs on Wednesday as long as the rain stays away. After that, I plan to go somewhere for a break.

Ten years ago I wrote a murky memoir called *A Gambler Born and Bred* while I was staying at the YMCA in Wimbledon after becoming homeless. This was when I was ostracised from my children by their mother. By writing I saw that constant struggles throughout my life had always been attributable to and made worse by my gambling. I posted chapters on a writers' website but didn't send it off to publishers. I recently looked to see if it was still on the site but it's not there. I'm too scared to look on my old laptop or various USB keys in case it's not there. There's a chance that the lady who runs the site has it lodged somewhere but I don't want to ask.

The mother of my children hasn't responded to emails that I've sent for months now. All I ask for is news on the girls but she's gone completely silent.

I fear that my eldest, who's now nineteen, has decided she wants nothing to do with me. My youngest is fifteen but I was never really allowed to bond with her so she probably regards me even more distantly.

I've never felt more alone. I've cut all contact with my three sisters and have no friends left. Of the few that had remained, one died of cancer a few months ago, another died a year ago and another died two years ago. One other friend has taken a step back because we feed each other's gambling addiction and the other two have told me to get lost and grow up after I got pissed/political with them. Everything's so divisive now. It doesn't help me seeing a married woman. People don't like that.

The lady has been a huge inspiration in my life for the last two and a half years. She's kept me buoyant and never judged me for my foibles, even when I've been painfully honest about my gambling. A year ago, when we went to see her therapist together and the day before I'd blown fifteen hundred on a spree, even then, she was kind and understanding.

A few weeks ago I went to stay at a past acquaintance's short stay rental flat in Hastings for the weekend. She'd posted on social media that the flat had become available so she did me a deal. I arrived on Friday afternoon, dumped my stuff off and then went to meet up with her by foot. She's been sober for a few years and it was good to see her looking so well. We had lunch somewhere and chatted about old friends mostly. I asked if she knew anyone who had any dope and she laughed, then I went off and found a bookies.

I didn't bet too much that day, flitting off to the pub at intervals and looking around the charity shops, familiarising myself with the place. The next morning, Saturday, I met up with her again and her dad gave me a few ready-rolled joints. He's an old head whose recent crop had been a disaster but he'd still scraped a few joints together for me.

It was bonfire night so we arranged to meet at six to enjoy the pagan procession through the town. Off I went to the bookies at midday. There was a pub round the corner to flit between the two all day, checking on runners and riders with a quickly drained pint. By about five I was a grand down, pissed and stoned. I knew I couldn't possibly go and meet my friend in such a state so I kept on gambling. I was down to my last three hundred and I needed a hundred for the rental so I placed a crazy bet of twenty-five pound each-way on two horses, one at 28/1 and the other at 50/1. It was the six o'clock race at a rain drenched Wolverhampton, a large field with about four nags vying for favouritism at 4/1. I'd already decided that if I lost I'd just get blind drunk somewhere and go back to the flat. To hell with bonfire night.

As luck would have it I hadn't written the odds on the slip so when the 28/1 won at 40/1 and the other one placed at 66/1 I was on cloud nine. That crazy bet won seventeen hundred quid. Even better, my winnings had to be put back on my card and wouldn't be available for a few days so it was out of harm's way plus I had just enough to give my friend the ton and go out drinking, which is what I did.

I got thrown out of the pub round the corner for smoking a joint in the garden so I went to a convenience store and got two bottles of Peroni, then walked about watching the procession in a drunken daze. At about midnight I started to walk back to the flat and on the way I heard loud music coming from under the promenade. It was a makeshift party with a DJ so I danced about like a lunatic till two then wobbled back along the prom.

In the morning I felt wretched. I must have had fifteen pints and as the clouds began to unfold with aspirin I started to piece together my shenanigans. I realised I'd lost a jumper that I'd bought for the lady. I couldn't remember where I left it, then I remembered going back to the bookies and asking the manager to keep hold of it for me till the morning because I wanted to go out and get pissed. As a gesture I'd given him a fiver to keep him sweet. Then I recalled a blurred conversation I'd had with my friend later in the night, apologising for not turning up earlier for the procession. The gist of it was that she'd cook eggs and bacon at her place, which was close to the flat I'd crashed at, and that I should get there for ten.

All I wanted to do was drive back home but I had to give her the money for the flat so I quickly went to the bookies to grab the jumper and then went over. She cooked breakfast, which I managed to keep down. I told her about my gambling habit. Understandably, she was less than impressed.

When I confessed about yesterday's crazy spree, she squirreled away the hundred quid I'd placed on the kitchen top. Gamblers have awful reputations for good reason but I stopped stealing when I was about twenty-five. That wasn't my style. When I told her I won about five hundred quid the day before, she said 'but it's still so sad'. She's a good sort.

Once home, after an arduous drive back, I spent the day recuperating on the sofa.

Now the pubs are back open I've found another one with an old school fruit machine. When I finish work I usually go down there and plug some money in with a few pints, then go to the bookies if I'm feeling the flavour. By and large this is how I spend my weekdays.

On the Saturday, which is unquestionably the loneliest day of the week without the kids and therefore the one I feel the most urgent need to gamble, I lost about a grand. I can't remember where but I got very drunk in the process. The Sunday after, I went up to Brixton to see the flat a second time for measurements and to talk through the exchange. I got there at lunchtime and they'd cooked something so they invited me to join them. They're a nice pair and we chatted till about three.

I planned on going into Brixton to find the best bookies and pubs for when I move but I was too hung over. I had a few bets riding on the footy so I found a local pub and watched it there. They had an old school fruit machine and I won the jackpot of a hundred quid but I'd put a hundred in. I had a pint and a half of Guinness and in that time the football bets I'd placed both lost so I got on my way, thinking I'd go home to lick my wounds, but when I was driving through Wandsworth I saw a BetFred so I stopped and went in there.

Liverpool were playing Man United at Old Trafford and I had a feeling they'd trounce it so I put a monkey (five hundred) on a Liverpool win. The match screen was all fuzzed up but you could just about see what was happening if you squinted. By half-time Liverpool were three up. I thought of cashing out but it was only offering a grand back. If I waited for the final whistle I'd get eleven hundred and fifty so I decided to hold out and found a pub just round the corner to watch the second half.

It was a lovely place with vibrant, happy staff and a good buzz so I supped down a few pints of Peroni and watched with glee as Liverpool went further ahead. They won five-nil in the end so I went back to the bookies and had the winnings placed back on the card, then I won another few hundred on dogs and virtual horses so I went back to the pub for a top up and then got on my way.

This last week's been a flurry of work and gambling and not much else. On the Tuesday I went to the bookies in Cranleigh and the guy there had come all the way from Seaford to replace the manager, who was off sick. There's a lot of young guys managing the bookies these days, disposable slaves on minimum wage and usually gamblers in the making. He needed to close early to get home in good time, a young father. There were roadworks and he was stressed out. I told him to cool it.

On Wednesday I went to a bookies in Godalming. I'd self-excluded from there a couple of years ago and the ban had elapsed. I tried to go back in a month ago but they told me I had to sign a form and that after twenty-four hours the self-exclusion would be void. This was the first time I'd been back and when I placed my first bet the young manager asked me to confirm that I was the guy who'd self-excluded so I told him yes. He just wanted to make sure, doing his job.

His assistant, a young, bright-eyed lad, had obviously been clued up on me (I'm known in most towns' betting fraternities as a pathological gambler, painter and drinker). He told me he'd lost six hundred quid at the other bookies down the road just the day before. We chatted about the hell we put ourselves through, knowing that the devil rests happily in our brain. Only we can remove him. All that bollocks.

All the time we're talking about the sickness I'm making crazy bets on outsiders. I won about six hundred quid that day.

Yesterday, Friday, I didn't work so I tried doing the right thing in the morning, going into town to sort a few things out. I found a lovely new cashmere jumper for the lady in a charity shop to go along with the other one I got in Hastings so that's her Christmas sorted. I also found *Natural Born Killers*, *Nil by Mouth* and *21 Grams* on DVD. After filling up the car and doing a brief shop for bottles of Warsteiner lager at the big Sainsburys I finally caved in and went to the pub for a few pints at lunchtime, then I went to the bookies at Bellfields.

I'd self-excluded from that one too about two years ago and I got found out about a week or two back by the lady manager so I went through the twenty-four hour thing. The staff now view me with vague suspicion so I never stay long. It's too close to home and they know I drive so I don't go in there steaming either.

This time, it was the young guy, Tommy, who seemed to view me with the most suspicion, and the manageress. There was a different atmosphere in the air when I walked in. I'd only had three pints so I was buoyant but not wide-eyed.

The manageress was upbeat when she saw me and reminded me that I'd given her one of my children's books about ten years ago. I'd completely forgotten so we sparked up a bit of a conversation about back then, when I lived up the road. The only thing I could remember about that bookies was when I won big on a horse called Writers Block at 50/1. You only remember the winners.

When she finished her shift, it was just me and Tommy. It turned out he's a gambler too, self-excluded from various bookies in town. He confided that he needed to get a different job because he was losing most of his wages to gambling one way or another. That was when I realised why he'd previously viewed me with such suspicion; he was looking at a mirror image of himself, an older, more decrepit version, someone he hated for what I represented in him. I told him that if he didn't get out of gambling it would ruin any decent relationships and may well kill him in the end through shame, destitution and guilt-riddled thoughts on repeat.

He told me he'd just been paid and only had sixty quid left to see him through the whole month. He'd paid his rent but gambling had swallowed everything else in one lager-fuelled Saturday afternoon. I told him to learn a trade and he said his dad could get him a job as a bricklayer. He has the perfect body to be a bricklayer, shortish but with big bone structure. I told him so. He showed me a picture of himself before working at the bookies, when he went down the gym and trained hard.

'Look at me now,' he said, getting up from his stool and presenting the belly.

'It's not about just getting a job, though,' I said. 'It's about application. If you apply yourself to a trade you'll make good money. Just get out of here and you'll be fine.'

I was there for a good few hours. Someone came in and played a machine but apart from that it was just us two.

I was losing big, probably close to a grand. I knew I'd lose when I drove there but it didn't stop me. I'd won all week and the weekends hadn't been too bad but I could feel where it was heading.

The British races had finished so it was onto the American ones. I totted up my losses and reckoned I was twelve hundred down and it was then that I saw a horse's name I couldn't resist. I still had a grand left in the account so I put four hundred on Born Gambler, a 2/1 favourite at Belmont Park in the six-thirty race.

It was a small field of six horses. Born Gambler took up his place behind the leading pack of three. Rounding the final turn he worked his way through the pack and in towards the rail. On the straight it was a two-way battle with both horses' necks pushed and shoved and cajoled in the men's firm hands. In the final furlong Born Gambler looked beat but then he pushed again and just snuck in front at the death.

I looked over to Tommy and his mouth was wide open. He should have had goggles on, his eyes were almost popping out. And that's why we bet - the adrenaline pumped, the testosterone in fever, the endorphins exploding in the brain.

I'd clawed back eight hundred and I knew I had to stop there. He said he'd give me cash but I asked for it to be put back onto the card to keep it out of harm's way. My stomach was screaming for food, I hadn't bothered eating all day, but I just couldn't seem to leave the place. The next race at Belmont had a horse called Always Gambling, an even firmer favourite at 10/11. I drew the horse's name to Tommy's attention and I could see the excitement in his eyes but I couldn't bring myself to bet. I was close to putting five hundred on but the following day was a Saturday and I wanted as much as possible to bet with.

We watched the race and it won by a good five lengths but I wasn't bothered. If I'd been on him I'd have been back at even terms and maybe a hundred ahead but hey ho. I said bye and drove home, heated up a fish pie and cracked open a litre bottle of Baileys to go with *21 Grams, Nil by Mouth*, passing out halfway through *Natural Born Killers*, the bottle dry.

It's now just gone one in the afternoon on Saturday. I know what I need to do; go to the bank and take out nine hundred quid so I can gamble without using the card. The card takes too long to process at the till, not good for a late bet.

The twelve hundred from Born Gambler probably won't be available till Monday so I'm set for the weekend. Arsenal are two up in the early kick-off against Leicester so my accumulators are in fine fettle. I know there's nothing else in my life, especially now the lady's not around. You may be crying out for me to stop, go take a nice walk in the countryside and have a hearty pub lunch somewhere decent. But you know that won't happen. Wish me luck, suckers.

*

It's Sunday morning and I've just had boiled eggs with soldiers. Sleep's been bad lately but that's down to my silence with the lady. It happens every time I split with a girlfriend, a few months of painful torment and then I'm usually right as rain. The big difference with this very fine lady is that I haven't screwed things up as I normally do, so it's not dead in the water. December 17th is the date we chose to see each other again, two days short of seven weeks from now.

There was a spider in the kitchen sink so I scooped it up and let it out of the window. It had been hanging out by the teabags for days, not moving an inch. I always thought spiders must be quite intelligent just sat there for days in mild contemplation but then you come back and find them in the sink or even the bath. I mean, why would they go into a place they know they can't get out of? Maybe it's a suicidal thing they have going on but whenever I go to fetch them out they're always very keen to comply. I suppose if there weren't any bookies or fruit machines about I'd be quite happy to comply too. It's a wet, grey, dark and windy morning so I felt bad putting him out.

Yesterday wasn't such a wild gambling day. Perhaps writing in the morning helped, I don't know. Oh, and I remembered what I did last Saturday. That was a messy one. I went to various pubs and I know I broke even because I had cash all week with untouched wedge still in the bank. The thing that made me recall events was going up to the manager of the only pub I still drink at in Guildford and telling him he's a mean old twat. He reminds me of a lizard and always puts too much froth on the pint. I'm sick of it.

They all do it now, it's a corporate trick saying it's the continental way when really they're just saving on the barrel. They even lie about the whereabouts of the pint line on a Peroni glass.

He came back with his trademark inch and a half froth on my pint so I asked for a flake. He sneered so I told him I only like head from a bird and asked him to fill it up. To be fair he did try to but there was still a good inch of fluff on the top. I stood at the bar to piss him off and I was in one of my tetchy moods when anything can happen. He was on his laptop as usual, sat at a table in the bar area, probably crunching numbers and sending pissy emails. They used to be landlords but not now; they're just email managers. Most would be better suited to a position in the prison service, young conservatives in the making, resentful that their youth had been stolen to pay a ten-year debt for the privilege of going to university in order to learn how to be a complete twat with no balls.

While I was standing at the bar, I started chatting to a blonde woman but her bloke came back from the toilet. I asked them what they were up to and they told me they were going to see a Smiths tribute band up the road. I know the place and it's easy to slip in through the back door once the gig's underway.

I went up to the manager and asked him why he'd always been offhand with me. He didn't say anything, just gave me a surly grin, so I told him he was a mean old twat and that he'd never see me in there again.

Off home, I had a pizza and a bottle of Warsteiner and then wobbled down to the venue. I snuck in through the back door and the band was really good so I started doing my stupid dance but it pissed off a young bloke and he tried to start a fight with me. I don't do that sort of thing unless I'm really pushed and as he kept shouting at me, spitting his fury in the middle of the dancefloor, I was sorely tempted to kick him in the balls and get it going but I kept thinking about the implant the dentist put in about six months ago for the princely sum of a grand. The thought of having to look for it on a lager-stained dancefloor saved the day and I walked away to get a drink at the bar. I stayed on for half an hour then went home and crashed on the sofa.

I threw up at about five, thanks to the two double Sambucas sloshed down earlier in the day. I can't mix my drinks. I can have ten pints and get away with it but if I have just one shot of Sambuca, I'm liable to chunder. That was the first puke in a very long while so not too shabby, all things considered.

Back to that crappy Saturday, I went to a country pub and had a couple of pints, then drove off to another one closer to an out of town bookies and drained a quick one there. Two isn't enough for a three-hour gambling session.

There was only one other guy there and he left after a few minutes. The old boy behind the counter asked how long I thought bookies would last as high street shops and I said about five years, which was about where he put it too.

No one goes to the bookies for racing anymore, not outside London anyway. There's the odd old boy who slowly fritters his pension away and then there's the crack dealer or builder rinsing notes at a machine, but by and large the shops are only really there for the problem gamblers who can't bet online because they've self-excluded. People like me. I chose a lifetime ban from all UK gambling websites to put an end to it once and for all, which has curbed the home-based gambling. But as long as there are bookies about I'll always want to take the liberty of going in and having a flutter after a few beers.

I was four hundred down so I put two hundred on a very firm favourite in a large field at Turffontein, a racetrack in South

Africa. All but one of my virtual bets had flopped and it was the same story with the British races. The favourite came in so I put fifty on another favourite in the next race and that came in too so I was two hundred up on the day, reducing my weekend loss to about five hundred. I had an accumulator going and two of the matches had come in but I needed Tottenham to beat Man United for the four hundred payout. That would have seen me almost even on the weekend but it didn't work out, with Man United trouncing Spurs three-nil.

I'm so tired of gambling. With nothing from the lady, my betting has escalated from silly little flutters to a daily grind that rules me with an iron rod. The drinking's increased because without that the gambling's pretty boring. I asked the gardener at the place I'm working if he knew anyone who sold pot and he said he'd ask around but he hasn't called yet. I like to think the pot keeps me away from the bookies but I always go in the end.

I'm not sure what I'll do today. I have a pulled pork thing so I could get some cabbage or kale and stock up on the vitamins but that's not exactly going to be a highlight for the day. I could go to the pub with the old school fruit machine but that's miles away and it'll probably be heaving as it's Sunday, which is a drag because the machine sits right between the front and the back of the pub so there's lots of traffic and I have to tuck myself in as people go past.

I forgot to say that when I was at the bookies that lost Saturday I got a call from a London number so I answered it.

It was Joan. Terry, my only known living relative outside of my immediate family, had died suddenly.

She'd called in the middle of a race and I felt terrible listening to her with one eye on a bunch of nags. Terry had died and I couldn't even tear myself away from a mares' novice at Towcester. Admittedly, I had a tenner each-way on an outsider but that was having the shit whipped out of its arse.

The funeral would be on the eighteen of November. Terry's

wife was in a bad way. At least she had Joan, who was now looking after her at home. I asked for her to pass on my best wishes and condolences and we hung up as the race ended, my horse nowhere.

Terry's father was the author of *A Hoxton Childhood*, a classic East End memoir that was first published in 1969. A S Jasper, the author, was the brother of my grandmother. Terry had known my father well as a child through to young adulthood but then they lost contact.

About ten years ago, Terry did a genes search and found my sister. I was trying my hand at publishing at that time and offered to make a reprint of the book with Terry. We sold about a thousand copies in the first year and got to know each other pretty well.

In *A Hoxton Childhood*, A S Jasper recounts his early life in a London slum before, during and after the First World War. His father (my great grandfather) was a raging alcoholic thief with a gambling habit. My grandma (the youngest of six children) is mentioned on the first page of the book, in a pram outside a pub on a Sunday night. The family moved from hovel to hovel when the feckless father couldn't pay the rent.

The author had visited my family at the time the book was first published by Barrie and Rockliff in 1969 but my grandma wanted nothing to do with it. She was ashamed of her past and her childhood had always been something she wanted to forget.

A S Jasper was saddened by his sister's refusal to accept the book's existence and he died soon after publication was met with the best of reviews.

I felt very sad that Terry had now gone.

*

It's been a horrendous week and it's now Saturday again.

On Tuesday I left the ladders leaning against the owner's bedroom balcony and she had to ask a neighbour to help take them down. Not good. Then I went and scored some hash from my new contact. Not good. Then I finished the job on Wednesday so I went for a drink then I went to the bookies and lost twelve hundred. Not good. On Thursday I did the same again.

On Friday, yesterday, I was too downtrodden to face the bookies, just got stoned all day. I did go and place a quick accumulator on the footy at sixish but that lost two hundred in the first ten minutes of play.

It always happens when there's too much money sloshing about. I just don't know what to do with it and such is my adamant sense of worthlessness the need to relieve myself of it is on me until it's gone, always with that crazy notion that I'll win enough to buy a house and stop for good. Now I'm down to four and a half thousand when I should be at eight. It's a disaster so I must at least try and win it back.

I have a habit of making vague plans to go away and write somewhere once work has dropped off, but that went out the window with the pot so I've been drinking, smoking and gambling outside of work. It's no way to live and I often revile myself. If the lady saw me she'd think I'd lost the plot completely. The guy I'm supposed to be exchanging with in Brixton texted on Wednesday to say the move has been declined because of his cat. We can appeal so let's see. I can't get in touch with my housing officer as her number has gone dead.

It's now the following Wednesday and I'm down to my last two grand. I'm in a state of barely manageable madness, knowing that I'll only feel better once the money's been drained. Gone is the new car I'd promised myself, the dreams of winning big smashed and replaced by the certainty of more loss.

I got drunk last night and finished off the hash, causing an unsettled night's sleep. I had a dream in which I was onto a sure winner and all I had to do was remember the name of the horse. I must have woken up twenty times with that name stuck in my head but I can't remember a thing now.

The madness stretches far further than that. When it's got you in its grip it won't let go until every penny has been passed over the counter and wasted. Only losing the lot can dismantle the cage, like starving yourself so you can finally wriggle through the bars and set yourself free.

There's no rhyme or reason to my betting. Over the past month I've ridden my luck with some big wins but they only served to keep me in the loop.

It's now Friday and almost all of the money I earned has gone. Eight grand. There's enough to pay the rent on Monday and I won't be dipping into that. When I look into the mirror I can't recognize myself. Maybe it's the new haircut but I'm scared.

I had a bit of work on Monday and Tuesday and I've been out gambling the rest of the week. I put five hundred on a long accumulator with about fifteen international teams to get back four thousand, all of which I thought would be surefire winners. In the early kick-off, Sweden, who are on top of one of the qualifying groups, were playing away to lowly Georgia, who had no chance of qualifying after five defeats from seven matches. At very short odds, I thought this would be a breeze for Sweden but somewhere in the back of my mind I feared an upset. They lost 2-0 so the bet was off from the start. I felt a certain lift knowing that the torment would soon subside but that lift was met with heavy, remorseful thoughts.

If I let those remorseful thoughts hang around long enough I'm liable to go into one of my depressive dips, which means I can't even get out of the flat. Work always dries up in winter and I know I'm in for a bumpy ride this year, especially if I'm moving. I have a week's work starting Sunday, which will pay for bills and food and roll ups.

It's easier when I don't have money. After a few weeks without a gamble I return to myself and get back on the horse to fight again, so to speak. There should be some work with Tony, too, so I can keep busy. It doesn't pay much working for other painters but at least it gives a sense of purpose, and it's generally good to work as part of his team. They're a decent bunch by and large.

I went out for a coffee in town this morning and became extremely morose as I sat in the little café contemplating my lot. The worst thought is that nothing will ever change, that I'll just keep bobbing up and down in my little sea of disquiet. I know that I'm the only one who can rescue the situation and find some stability. Help's an inside job.

I can't use the absence of the lady as an excuse to fritter my money away so senselessly. It's been thirty-three days since I last saw her and in that time my gambling has spiraled out of control. To be frank, it was pretty bad when I was seeing her but at least she gave me something to look forward to every week, a bit of buoyancy. With her gone there's nothing to stop me wreaking havoc. I texted her brother to ask how she was and he told me there's no change but she's bearing up ok, all things considered. I felt marginally better knowing this but there are still thirty-four days until I next see her. I'm halfway there but even then there may be no movement with another mountain of time to climb.

We've talked about the possibility of being together as a real couple and I told her of my plan as far as gambling was concerned. All my wages would be transferred into an account in my name that only she could withdraw from. I would be given a certain amount to live on independently. It's a bit like pocket money, though, and she's not keen on the idea but there's no cure for gambling. Only prevention, or damage limitation, can steer me away from the dreaded bookies and fruit machines.

I saw a television documentary on gambling a few weeks

ago. In it, Paul Merson, who was a massive football hero for me back in the eighties and nineties, recounted how he lived on pocket money from his wife. Only the year before he'd blown the deposit for a house, which would have given his family a much greater sense of stability. He estimated that he'd frittered away about seven million quid during his life and he was honest enough to say that gambling would always be with him, that it would never leave him or let him go. His addiction to alcohol and cocaine were a walk in the park compared to gambling and it struck a chord how the effects of these addictions compared against my own plight.

With booze and drugs your body will refuse further intake after a certain time, while with gambling you can blow millions and still seem fine on the surface. There's no staggering around blind drunk or heart seizures to stop you in your tracks at a few hundred quid and I suppose that's why one in three chronic gamblers commits suicide, because it's the only way out of the torment.

If I take the birthday of my seventh year on the planet as my first experience of gambling, next year will be my fiftieth year as a pathological gambler. That first visit to The Bright Spot in New Brighton was my earliest memory in life and I can still see the place in my mind right now.

I looked it up on the net and it's been renamed 'The New Palace and Adventureland', describing itself as 'a fantastic entertainment area with a variety of machines to suit all ages from toddlers to young-at-heart grandparents'.

When I was about nine, say 1974, I was already well into my gambling odyssey, thieving money from wherever I could to feed the machines at The Bright Spot. At around this time, I found out that the population of Britain stood at about fifty million.

My favoured machine at The Bright Spot was The Penny Falls (similar to The Tipping Point on telly) and my currency for betting was a 2p coin. When I learnt about the population of

Britain, about 50 million, I made a calculation that if everyone in Britain gave me 2p each, I'd have a million quid to gamble with. From the desperation of my poisoned mind I'd inadvertently invented a form of the lottery!

Back to the lady, who I really do, unfortunately, love. She's a life liver; she enjoys the daily art of living on life's terms and she's a high achiever in whatever she does, be that mothering, working or partying. She's as free a person as I've ever met and that's why I call her a life liver.

When I said this to her she wasn't convinced. She also has issues with self-worth but they're manageable compared to mine and she's found constructive ways to defend her right to a good life.

I described myself to her as a life survivor because I'm always at war with myself. Money is my ammunition and the bookies and pub machines make up the battleground but my only real enemy is me. It's very sad.

Did I tell you that I haven't seen my children for twelve years? You're probably thinking it's a blessing they don't have to put up with me and I'd agree to an extent. I've always loved my children but I was never cut out to be a dad.

I've wanted to write a book about my removal from their lives but it's still too difficult. Every time I try, I go into such a morose state of mind that it disables me completely. The plan is that if I can write about my gambling, that sense of usefulness may return and help me write about my children. I still have the paperwork from the court case.

Their mother has ceased to reply to my emails for some months so I've finally got in touch with a lawyer in Berlin, whose contact details were given to me by a guy I did a job for. I have enough money stashed with the lady to pay him to find out how the children are and I'm hoping that he can find a way to reestablish contact.

Another positive aspect of my otherwise lacklustre life is that, earlier this week, I finally plucked up the courage to look for my murky memoir, *A Gambler Born and Bred*. It was still on the old Toshiba laptop.

*

It's now two weeks since I last wrote. For the last three years I've had a bill for an overpayment of housing benefit looming over me like a dark cloud. I could have paid it back ten times over but for a mixture of resentment and stupidity. Maybe in the back of my mind I knew I'd gamble the lot so I'd have to get in touch with the lady to ask her to let me have some of the money.

Whatever it is, the move to Brixton can't go ahead till the overpayment has been paid back so I did get in touch with her and thankfully she was kind enough to transfer enough to pay it off.

I asked how things were with her and she told me it's been hell. I told her about my gambling and that I've been drinking too much and she thinks I'm destroying myself. She asked, if I can't be kind to myself, how can I be kind to others? I couldn't argue with that but told her I'm doing my best, which is admittedly crap. We miss each other but both know she has to find resolution at home so we agreed that I'd text her closer to Christmas to see if we can at least exchange presents and go for lunch somewhere. That time is exactly three weeks away from now and I count the days, even when I know it may not happen.

The cat problem was solved after the housing association was told the full story, that she's sixteen years old and well into her retirement, a housecat that poses no problem to neighbours.

Once I'd got rid of all my money a fortnight ago and paid the benefit back, I started making small daily wins and walking away. This accumulated to about a grand. I talked to the lady and she urged me to get back in touch with the National Problem Gambling Clinic in London, where about four years ago I took part in group therapy. It had been a real help for a while but then I slid back into old habits.

The thing about self-worth is reward. If you're a high flyer with few emotional problems, you'll buy yourself a nice car that mirrors your own perceived value. Sooner or later you'll build your little empire and feel a sense of propriety that best befits your conformity to conventionally accepted standards of behaviour.

My self-worth acts in much the same way. As I feel utterly worthless I'll go to great lengths to mirror that sense of unimportance. The first reward after a hard day's work is lager. The sugar content raises my energy in the same way as I seek for the dope to deplete it. The second reward is gambling. After a few sherbets my mind is falsely freed from the shackles of despair so I'll waddle into a bookies and that takes care of the financial side, making me as worthless as I feel.

Yesterday I finally plucked up the courage to email the clinic and someone got back to me straight away with a form to fill in. As I couldn't fill it in online because of a glitch I called up the clinic and spoke to someone who told me that, because of restrictions, the group therapy sessions weren't available. I flipped. I was a bit rude and asked why having eight people in a well aired room discussing their innermost anxieties and trauma with those in similar circumstances wasn't permitted when eighty thousand people could cram into a stadium to spit fury and watch people kick a ball around. She agreed that it wasn't right and asked me to send an email explaining my qualms so that she could pass it on to the trustees. I did that this morning but it won't change a thing. She probably won't even reply. I often wonder if they're in cahoots with the Gambling Commission.

In the email I explained that I wouldn't be pursuing my

enquiry for help until the group therapy sessions were back on. Sadly, after that phone call yesterday, which I made in the pub, I went out and blew five hundred in anger.

It's the first of the month today so I paid my council tax and now I'm down to about four hundred. Although I intend to hang onto it the monkey on my back is already telling me to get off the computer and stop writing so I can go out and have a few beers and make some shrewd investments at the bookies. It's Tuesday and there's no work about apart from Friday, a flash coat on kitchen cabinets in Barnes for Tony.

I bumped into my gambling buddy, Kieran, the other day. He was smashed. Like me, he can't really take his drink and for some reason he kept calling me a self-centred, puritanical cunt. He also told me how he'd opened an account with a building society where he had to apply for his money and wait three months to take it out. I'd previously urged him to find a way to do this but could I do it for myself? No.

He hadn't brought his card out so I lent him twenty quid and got a round in, then he told me about his first ever gamble.

He was fourteen years old. He'd saved some of the paper round money and wanted to buy himself a bike. His dad was a proper hard case gambler and a horse of interest was running somewhere so Kieran decided to place a bet of twenty pounds each-way on the horse, called Worldly Lad. It came in at 7/1 and that was it for poor old Kieran.

As you may recall, Kieran is my only friend now. Even my lady friend in Chiswick has closed ranks. I have lots of acquaintances but none that I can or want to confide in. Every time I've done so in the past I've left with an awful feeling of vulnerability. In a way Kieran and I try to help each other through the worst times. We don't gamble together any more. When he loses I can feel a punch coming my way if I have a little dig.

I went to Terry's funeral last week with my sister and her husband. We went in his car. That was the first time I'd seen that sister in over a year and we got on well. The funeral was in Chingford and some bird pinched my bum at the wake. Girls are funny at wakes and weddings.

It's now one-thirty. The racing is underway and I'm sat here writing but my heart's not in it so I'll stop for a while, maybe go and make those shrewd bets. My stars said I'd have some luck this week but yesterday, Monday, wasn't exactly the best start although in my sick mind I can easily put that down to the call with the National Problem Gambling Clinic.

This is how I lost the five hundred. I'd been drinking at a pub close to the Betfred in Godalming and I was about evens. All I had to do was get back to the car, which was at the other end of the high street, and go home.

As I approached the Coral, from which I'd self excluded many years ago and never gone back, I decided to go in and chance it with Nick, the server of ten years. I said hello and asked if I could have a flutter. He asked if I was still self-excluded so I told him no and that was carte blanche.

I got on a machine, making hasty bets on the horses at intervals. At one point, about four hundred down, I went outside for a fag and a chat with Nick, who's also a smoker, and when I went back in I found a guy on my machine playing with my money. I berated him and he lied, saying he thought I'd left, but he paid me back the eleven quid and vacated the machine for me to plug some more.

He was one of three delivery guys. They'd come over to Blighty for a better life, only to put all their hard earned wages down the gullet of those dreadful machines.

My last bet was a hundred on a horse called Global Connection. It was in the lead until the final throes, when a rank outsider came steaming past and kissed it on the line. That was my first win-only bet all day, another typical twist in the lashing tail of horse racing that whips you on the legs just when you think you're winning.

I don't know which bookies to use today. The one in Farncombe (my least lucky bookies) closed down for good the other day. That's the way it's going now that the online side is so lucrative. There's no rent or rates to pay but they have to keep the bigger shops going for the guys like me who have self-excluded for life online.

There are half a million 'problem gamblers' in the UK and we represent only 5% of all those who gamble, which means there are ten million gamblers in the country. It's thought that the 5% problem gamblers represent 86% of all gambling revenues so they have to find ways of reeling us back in if the online market is out of bounds. But there's no use me wishing for all bookies to close up for good. It'll never happen.

With no work until Friday I woke up on Wednesday and was bored stiff in an instant so I went to London for a sup and a flutter in Soho. I should have been concentrating on clearing out unwanted artwork and decluttering the flat for the move but the urge for a flutter was too strong. The pub in Cranleigh that has my favoured fruit machine's still closed for some reason and I spent Monday and Tuesday at various second rate pubs and bookies, spilling bits of cash I can barely afford to lose.

I hadn't been to Soho for about six weeks so I was quite excited on the way up in the car. The new ultra low emissions scheme has come into effect and I wanted to see how easy it would be to park on Putney Hill, which is just outside the south circular, where the scheme starts. £12.50 to drive your car around inner London seems a real rip off but with the world going to pot I suppose something needed cooking up. My car's an old diesel Audi and I can't stand the thought of letting it go. Even worse is the prospect of having to swap it for a Nissan Note or a bloody Honda Jazz.

Parking was a breeze so I walked down the hill and ducked into Tesco for a pack of rollies and a couple of lottery tickets for Friday's super jackpot draw, then I went to Paddy Power with an old betting slip I couldn't remember had won or not. It paid seventeen pound fifty so I pocketed that and got on the number fourteen bus into town. Masks are compulsory again but there was hardly anyone on the top deck so I watched the world go by with it hanging off an ear till about South Kensington, when it filled up.

While my mask was still off I saw my old gambling buddy's girlfriend at a bench on the Fulham Road. He died two Christmases ago. I tried to keep in touch with her afterwards but she was rude to me in Soho when I was drunk so I deleted her number.

She was sat at that bench, masked up and with her trademark bobble hat on. To one side was a massive, bulging suitcase on wheels and on the other side was a smaller but still heavily laden holdall. This was odd because she's got a flat close by. Before that, she'd been homeless with my mate for a good decade and now here she was again, with her bags, sat at a bench. I was sure it was her.

I didn't wave but she definitely clocked me and I wondered what sort of trouble she'd got herself into. I care about her but I've cut my ties now so that's that. I wonder if she's finally going back to South America. Who knows?

The traffic was a drag in Knightsbridge as usual but before and after was fine. I got off at the Curzon Soho and made my way to the pub to get tanked up for a flutter. Once I'd downed a couple of pints I headed off to the bookies in Chinatown, only a few minutes' walk. My luck wasn't great so I left after an hour or so. Down to my last hundred and fifty quid and with no work apart from a piddly kitchen makeover in Barnes, it was make or break time again.

I took out eighty quid from the cashpoint and went to the Betfred down the road to see if a new setting could wriggle some winners my way but again my luck was out. I had fifty quid left in the bank and eighty in the wallet.

On the way to the first bookies I spotted an old school fruit machine in one of the other pubs so I went there and started plugging it with a consolatory Peroni. It was a Casino Crazy machine, a good, reliably entertaining machine with the mega streak option.

It's quite easy to tell if a machine's in a good mood and I quickly realised things were looking up as the mega streak percentage went up and up till it got to 150%, which is where it stops until it pays out the jackpot. The trick is not to take low offers like twenty-five quid. If you do that the mega streak percentage goes back down to zero and you have to start building it up again, which can take anything from fifty to a hundred and fifty quid, which I didn't have.

Forty quid and two pints in, the mega streak paid out the princely sum of one hundred and ten quid. It came out in pound coins so I had to get the manager down from his slumber to convert it into notes and he told me that was the first time the jackpot had paid out in over a year. I told him about my trick of holding out for the mega streak but he wasn't really interested. I was by then quite animated and high on beer and the adrenaline of winning, which is when I start talking to strangers. I met a lovely old Scottish couple and we chewed the fat about lockdown for a while, then I went off to a pub I hadn't been to for a good few years and happened upon a gorgeous woman there.

I ordered a pint and decided to smoke my rollie in the pub, which completely foxed the lovely lady. She asked how I could have the gall to do it and I told her that staff don't usually mind, that it's such a benignly disobedient thing to do that they feel obliged to turn a blind eye. Mind you, on a plane, if someone smoked a fag they'd probably reroute the thing to a military base and incarcerate the smoker.

Sadly her husband appeared a few moments later. He gave me the evils but the girl introduced me and we got on fine. I left telling the guy how lucky he was to have her and guaranteed that she'd never leave him in a million years as long as he treated her right.

I was in such a good mood that I went back to the Betfred and put a tenner on the nose of a virtual horse called Viva Nothing with odds of 10/1. The name made me laugh my head off; Long Live Nothing, a very topical choice of names probably made up by a quirky, nihilistic Scouser in Gibraltar.

Viva Nothing pipped the favourite at the post and paid out a hundred and ten quid so I wobbled off and took the tube back to Putney Bridge. The journey on the bus in had taken about an hour and I didn't want to get cut short.

Having had nothing to eat all day I stopped off at the Eight Bells and ordered a rib eye with all the trimmings. Aware that I was a bit worse for wear I amazed myself by ordering only half a pint.

Once I'd polished that off, I took the bus up the high street and just as I got to the car, my painting buddy Tony texted to say there's some indoor work for me next week at a house close to the flat, which really is a game changer as I've got rent to pay the week after and I don't want to contact the lady for another slice of my savings.

It must have been about 9pm by then. Over the period of seven hours I reckon I'd had five and a half pints.

I was still in a great mood so I put some music on and got going. The A3's an easygoing route out of London. At Putney Vale it's forty miles an hour and then there's a stretch with a fifty mile an hour limit till you get far out enough for the seventy mile an hour stretch.

I'm usually really good and patient when I know I'm over the limit but I was in such high spirits I couldn't help passing the forty mile an hour brigade just at the point it turns into a fifty zone just after the Robin Hood roundabout. I was doing just shy of seventy when I clocked a police car laying in wait up ahead. I slammed on the brakes but the damage was done; they'd seen me coming.

I kept to a steady fifty and then I saw the blues in the rear-view mirror. They were right up my arse so I pulled into the slip road to Raynes Park and lowered my window. The police car came alongside. The officer in the passenger seat told me to get off the slip road so he could have a word. I was shitting my bricks but I'm quite good in a tight spot.

This was the first time I'd been stopped in at least twenty years and strangely enough the last time I got done was by camera for speeding, just on the opposite side of the A3 from where I was. That must have been a good six years ago and I'd opted for the speed awareness course to save on the insurance and the three points. I've had a clean licence for about thirty years and I suppose I pride myself on my driving, even with everything you know about my habits. Having been in plenty of death defying scrapes over the years I've never once actually caused an accident, although I've certainly come close on one or two occasions.

I carried on and indicated to go into the mega Next car park. Once there I turned off the engine and waited for one of the officers. When he came to stand at my door I got out and he asked for my licence, telling me he'd clocked me doing sixty-eight in a fifty. I dug my hand into my pocket and quickly dispatched my licence to him. He asked me to sit in my car while he went back to his to do some checks. Those five or so minutes seemed like an eternity.

When he came back I got out again and he gave back my licence. I was all coy and desperate to show remorse so I had the pursed, upturned lower lip on, avoiding eye contact but briefly and intermittently looking to him as he spoke. Quickly enough, he told me that I may or may not receive a letter in the post for the offence. I didn't ask any questions, just said ok and thank you and then he turned and walked back to his car.

I couldn't believe my luck. In those excruciating few minutes I'd foreseen my future; an out of work painter with no wheels, forced onto public transport to agency jobs with a backpack for equipment, when work appeared. Then I saw the looks on customers' faces as I arrived, a mess. Sure, I could buy materials and have them delivered but I've hardly ever been without a car all through my adult life, even in Paris. And what about the step ladders and the roller pole?

The thought of having to take public transport everywhere was beyond horrendous. If the move to Brixton went ahead I'd find it hard to get back down to Surrey for work without wheels. Trains and buses flashed through my mind, the only bonus being that I wouldn't have to pay for the upkeep of the car.

The police car followed me out from the mega Next car park but the road signage at the junction was so poor I couldn't tell whether I could go right to get back onto the A3. Not wanting to get out and ask the policeman, I indicated left and saw the police car go right, so I found a spot to do a U-turn and got on my way.

The journey back was mixed with woeful remorse and deep introspection. I kept a keen eye on my speed and stayed within the limit the whole way, discerning that this would be my new driving etiquette. I just can't afford to lose my licence and it felt like a real lesson learnt, having avoided a drink drive ban under the trained nose of what appeared to be a very astute traffic officer. Maybe he'd just taken pity on me and let me off, I don't know.

It's now the next day, Thursday. I had a crap sleep but there was a spring in my step when I got up. I made some breakfast and then decided to get shot of a load of paintings that I don't really like, along with a few boxes of children's books.

I did four trips to the car, piled the stuff in and drove off to the charity shop on the high street that sells second hand artwork.

When I got there I showed the lady a few pictures and she said they were 'quite crazy' but she was happy to take them. She doesn't take books so I went to Oxfam with them. There was a note on the front door saying they weren't taking any donations but I went in and spoke to the manager, who agreed to take them in.

One of the volunteers in the back room asked about the kids' books and I told her I'd written them. I signed one for the manager's son and another for the volunteer's daughter. She asked if I was famous and I told her no, but that one of the books had done quite well at bookshops a few years ago, but then things changed at Waterstones and they stopped independent author signings. That was when the whole thing fell off a cliff.

It seemed strange talking about the books again, remembering the good old days before the big boys squeezed the little guys out of the market. At least I got to enjoy the tail end of the free world.

I dropped off the car at home and wandered into town with the express wish of going to another charity shop where I'd donated a whole load of books, DVDs and CDs the week before. In amongst that lot was a box set of *The Godfather* and I wanted to ask if I could borrow it back because, typically, I'd just seen the first in the trilogy on telly on Monday night. I was desperate to watch the other two so I went back there but I couldn't bring myself to ask so I went to the supermarket and got some shallots and cream to make a gratin to go along with some trout, a little treat for this afternoon.

Once home I automatically thought of finding out if the pub in Cranleigh with the fruit machine was back open but my little brush with the law last night put paid to that and I deleted the idea as nonsense, miraculously pondering over the possibility of actually reconfiguring how I live. It's probably fifty-fifty whether I get a letter from the police asking me to pay a fine or go on another bloody speed awareness course but I'm resigned to deal with it pronto if it comes. I still can't believe he didn't ask me to blow into the reader being so close to Christmas. Kieran had only the day before told me they were out and about but I hadn't listened. When he was getting done for DD for the sixth time, the judge told him he'd most likely be sent down if he did it again so he's ultra rigid with his new driving system now.

I'm painfully but gratefully aware that I just missed a bullet by the skin of my teeth. From being in a great mood, listening to music with a full tummy and at worst a ton up on the day, my rude awakening has had the desired effect.

I've just popped the gratin in the oven and the trout is in a pan on a low heat but my mind is full of the lady. On Sunday, after a brief catch up call on the phone on Friday, she texted me out of the blue to say she missed me but that I mustn't reply. Such is our silence; we long to see each other. I've held off from replying till just now, when I texted to say I dream of holding her and kissing her and looking into her eyes. It was an impulsive decision but it's horrible being without her.

I wolfed down the trout and gratin and received a text from her; 'That's beautiful. Thank you. I do too x (don't answer)'.

There's no two ways about it; I need to really get a grip on my life. I'll be up dark and early tomorrow to get to Barnes by eight and it'll be my first time paying the new ultra low emission people. It's only about two hundred yards inside the south circular but beggars can't be choosers.

*

I did it again yesterday, a laughable, risible, idiotic Wednesday gamble full of conceited bravado. I was working for Tony on a crap job full of tradesmen trying to get past me while I painted door frames.

Someone got a phone call. His brother's a horse trainer, apparently. A few people got talking and word was that there were two horses to look out for in the afternoon's racing.

Just before lunchtime I asked if I could go and place a few bets and Tony said yes so I scampered off to the car and drove to what I thought was the closest bookies but it had closed permanently, then I drove to another part of town but they'd shut down too so I went to the Betfred in Bellfields. Tommy was there.

I did a twenty pound each-way double on the two horses, then two twenty pound each-way singles on both horses, a total investment of one hundred and twenty with a maximum payout of just over a grand. I wolfed something down at a café before going back.

Back in work mode, I heard the race with the others on someone's phone and the thing came third. It was a seven-horse race so it didn't even place. Two of my bets were already losers.

The second race was at cleaning up time but again we lost, coming fourth in a field of ten and hence out of the frame by the same margin as the other nag.

I'd called Kieran in the morning and told him about the tip so he'd downed tools and gone into Godalming to have a drink and a bet. He put a little less on than I did and we planned to meet for a drink before I headed home so I picked him up outside the bookies and we went off to the pub.

He was livid.

'I've watched horses since I was five years old and I tell you those jockeys did fuck all to win that.' In each of the races they'd given the leader a twenty-length advantage from the start. 'You'd have to be Frankel to win from that margin,' he said, utterly disgusted. He was quite pissed from an afternoon's drinking but still pretty animated. I had a couple there and then scarpered.

*

I moved to Brixton about a month ago and it's now 2022!

The speeding fine (£100) came in the post as I knew it would and I've been given my first points (three) in about thirty years. The little money I had has all but been squandered on the move. The lady likens her view of my situation to watching a car crash in slow motion. I laughed when she said that. I mean, what can you say?

We met up at about the time of the move, just after Christmas, but it's still tough at home for her. It sometimes seems as if there'll never be resolution. It's a crap state of affairs. The gambling has become so bad that I can't see I'll be a good partner for her anyway so I've gone into martyr mode, waiting to be put out of my misery by behaving as recklessly as I can. That pension pot came to sixteen hundred quid in the end. I blew it in three days.

The move was a nightmare and I feel drained of energy but that's probably more from the amount of alcohol and cannabis I've been using. That said, I've done all the changes of address with everyone. I still don't have a fridge and the oven was only connected last week so I've been on takeaways and generally eating badly. It's so much easier getting into bad habits than good ones and I'm no good at change.

When I finally put the washing machine to good use yesterday, it leaked from where I yanked at the hose to make sure it had been fitted properly. A towel on the floor was an adequate stopper but I can't use the thing until I get a new hose.

The local bookies provides me with the grass contact, and a pub close to the flat serves a decent five percent lager for just shy of four quid. A double Amaretto is a very reasonable fiver. I don't drink Sambuca any more.

The new flat is on the first floor of a period 1930s council block. One downside to the location is that it's just inside the new ultra low emission zone so every time I go out in the car it's costing me £12.50 a day. I pay online but it's eating into my weekly funds. Since the new year I've been working for Tony, which means crap pay but it's better than nothing plus he deducts income tax so my bill at the end of the year is much more manageable. If I'd bought a petrol car when I had the money I'd be clean as a whistle but because the Audi's an old diesel I get to pay Transport for London through the nose while they spew their fumes all over town. It does seem odd that the biggest polluter in the whole country charges those who can't afford to upgrade their vehicles. Tube stations and bus hubs have the highest recordings for emissions nationwide but that seems to have slipped the mind of the mayor, who reckons it's better for poor people to get ripped off on public transport than in their cars.

Back in November I had eight grand in the bank and six thousand four hundred with the lady but that's all gone. I had dreams of buying a respectable little petrol car but now I'm wondering whether I should just get rid of the Audi and work for agencies in London. Public transport links are pretty good here but as soon as you go near TfL it stinks to shit. The air's brimming with toxins in the tube.

Last Saturday I went to my first march in Britain. I arrived at the BBC building just north of Oxford Circus an hour early so I went around to the backstreets and found a nice little pub to have a few sharpeners. When I got back a massive crowd had built up and we all started making our way down to Trafalgar Square. I realized I'm not much of a marcher when I dipped into a pub in Carnaby Street and had a pint of Peroni. When I got on my way again about half an hour later, Regent Street was still full of marchers.

I walked down to Soho and had a go on the fruit machine at The Golden Lion, where I won the mega streak again, then it was off to Chinatown to see how my luck was. I lost the three hundred quid I'd just been paid in under an hour. That was supposed to pay for council tax and rent at the new flat.

A funny thing happened while I was licking my wounds with a pint and a roll up at The Coach and Horses. (It turned out that it was here that Bernard was most famous for his drinking banter.)

Sat at a stool outside, a loud hissing noise erupted from the back end of a theatre. It sounded like an air or gas leak and in under five seconds everyone apart from me had run off in different directions, fearing it to be a bomb. I watched the quietly managed mayhem with a smile and waited for the bang. It felt like as good a time as any but the bang never came.

There was a police van parked up only a few yards away so I had a word with them and asked if there'd been any trouble with the march.

'Not a peek,' one of them said.

'Hardly surprising, it's a peaceful protest.'

I went to another pub, pissed and lairy, asking a few of the punters for their favourite numbers so I could go back to the bookies with someone else's luck. The answers that came back were something like 23 and 14 so I asked for single numbers, hoping for a 7 and then forgetting what they said as I waddled back to the bookies. I couldn't get 7 out of my head all the way there but when I walked in I totally forgot my game plan and failed to book the 7 horses in the next two virtual races. They both won at silly odds and that's when I remembered the game plan so I stuck a hundred that I could barely afford on the 7 horse in the next race at Bath. It won at short odds so I waddled off and found another pub for a few final beers, then I caught the tube home.

One big difference about living back in London is the journey home. No more driving and the tube only takes fifteen minutes to get to Brixton, then it's a two-minute bus ride up the hill.

I've found a few pubs in the local area but my pattern of

behaviour has taken a turn for the worse. With none of my own work coming in, my funds are right on the edge and I'm constantly having to save and scrape to pay the rent every Monday. It's Monday tomorrow and I'm one pound short so I'll have to go to the bank in the morning and plonk it in.

The lady has been very sweet. I was in such a horribly low place yesterday that I texted not to see her as planned. She called up and after a good half an hour of deliberation she asked if she could come over and I said yes. We went out briefly to look at a second hand furniture shop and for soup and bread for lunch at the flat. She's really worried about me and feels powerless to help. I try my best to allay her fears because I know she cares. She's the spiritual type, no militant, just a kind, naturally caring person with a strong desire to have fun with everyone in her world.

It's Monday morning now. I did it again yesterday, with the rent money. That's the lowest of the low in terms of desperate measures and I'm feeling awful, sighing and huffing as the wind blows hard outside. There's a beautiful blue sky but it's a brash wind, the kind that makes you cry when you go into it. That's exactly how I feel about the day ahead so I've had a few small joints with my coffee. There's no work on the go so I'll sit and write down my traumatic, pathetic little existence.

Yesterday morning I had a nice chat with the lady on the phone while she was walking. She knows I have a propensity to stay in all day when there's no work, especially at weekends when I'm broke. She wanted me out and about, not to the pub, so I promised I'd go for a walk in Brockwell Park. It was too beautiful a day to stay in.

I spent about twenty minutes there, hideously self-conscious with all the happy or unhappy families and couples darting around. It's got a nice view over London but parks always make me feel isolated, like I'm in a bubble, so I got out quick. After taking a short cut through some back streets I found myself at the bookies. With forty-five quid in notes and one hundred and twenty in the bank I had enough to pay the rent and buy roll ups and food.

But I got a tenner bag, then I placed a few quid bets on nags and exited for the pub, rolling a wee joint for on the way. As soon as I got three pints down me I knew I'd have another bet and it would have to be with the rent money, which is due today. I went to the other pub for one more then breezed back into the bookies and blew the lot in under ten minutes. Two dogs and a virtual horse had found me out.

I went back to the pub for one more then got a potato, an onion, a bottle of Peroni and a pint of milk from the convenience shop. I had some tinned tuna at the flat so I put something together and then got stoned in front of the box.

I should get in touch with a sister to see if I can borrow a hundred and fifty. It will be the first time in a decade I've had to do anything like that but I'm at breaking point and there's no other solution. If I don't pay the rent I'll be out on my heel.

The lady just texted asking if I'd thought of anti-depressants so I reminded her that I'd tried them once in 2010 but they made me feel suicidal so she laid off that. Conversation always seems to wind back to me somehow finding help for my problems, which usually only serves to exacerbate the futility of it all. My main problem is that I haven't seen my kids for twelve and a half years. The lady calls it a 'living loss'.

She offered three ways of trying to make contact; email again to the lawyer (who hasn't replied), email again to the mother (who hasn't replied for months and months), and call the embassy. I added to call the FCO over here might help too, so it was a four-pronged attack.

But the fact is I'm scared I'll hear terrible news about my daughters, that that has been the reason their mother hasn't replied to my emails for so long.

It's now Wednesday. The lady came over yesterday and we

went for a walk in Brockwell Park, then had a light lunch at a pub in Brixton. It was good to see her and I felt lucid, free from the shackles of gambling thanks to my abject pennilessness. It's a catch 22 situation, a self-imprisonment.

I let her pay for lunch and kept it down to a starter and a pint of bitter. We shared some chips. It was a Young's pub anyway, which does crap food on the whole. After that, we walked back up the hill and took a coffee at the little Portuguese place.

'Is it doing you any good, though, writing this journal?' she asked cagily.

I said I didn't know but I couldn't stop now. I was enjoying the ride. Maybe I'd get clean and sober and stop gambling. Maybe that would be the conclusion of the book. Either way I'd need to finish it.

She asked to see it so I told her I'd send it to her as soon as it was done. She'd be the first to read it for sure. I only needed a few more months' material to get it over the line, etc.

The truth is, I can't stand the thought of her reading this.

She lent me forty quid, which I still have today. There's a certain change for the better in my outlook and I have to say that she always peps me up when I see her. Usually, on parting, I go straight to the pub and then waddle off to the bookies but not this time.

I've got to go to Surrey today to rectify a few small mistakes at a job I did a while back. Then I'm off to quote for a job near Guildford.

I called Kieran and asked to borrow a hundred so I'll meet him at a pub somewhere once he's finished work. If I get the job and it's quite sizeable, I'll be back in the game.

To be honest, I'm bored shitless of the pubs and the bookies but trying to find a sense of purpose when you're a lonesome fifty-six year old house painter isn't easy. The writing has been a real positive in many ways, destructive in others.

I still do the lottery and I know it's a crazy dream but someone has to win the damn thing. My dream is to buy a building and fill it with the best young minds that want to do away with scams and political skullduggery, exposing tyranny on a grand scale. The shysters would do all they could to stop us but we wouldn't go without a fight, plus I could look after myself in court with money behind me for when they got tasty. I'd live at the top of the building and have a helicopter for a quick exit. But then the lottery's probably a scam too.

I just took a call from Tony. He's got three more kitchens that need a flash coat so things are looking up. All I need to do is replace the Audi for a petrol banger and I'm set for the year.

I went down to Surrey to tidy up those loose ends at the job in Weybridge and got to the job in Bramley by three. It was a large Victorian house, pebbledash around the first floor and brickwork around the ground floor. The woodwork was in an atrocious state and when I gave the woman my price I could see her discomfort.

After that I met Kieran, who gave me the ton, then it was off to Cranleigh to get some pot, stopping for a couple at the pub with the fruit machine and returning back to Brixton by eight. Where would I be without a car? On the dole, that's where.

The next day, yesterday, I got up and decided to go to Tate Britain to look at art.

I left at about ten-thirty and walked down the hill, stoned from a morning's smoking and drinking coffee. Sat on the tube I reminded myself that I must leave £12.50 in the bank account to pay the bloody ULEZ charge.

Tate Britain's really changed. It used to be so much fun walking up the steps to the grand entrance but they've closed that off and built a walkway to the side that goes down into the basement of the building. It feels like you're walking into a rich man's morgue, the sterile reception area devoid of life.

Back in the 80's I used to drive the old Austin to Tate Britain of an afternoon with a girlfriend or a friend. There was usually a parking space on an old meter in the crescent that led directly to the steps up to the museum. I'd put two 50p pieces in, then stride up to the art. Nowadays, just being in a car in central London costs almost a score a day, parking can cost a ton a day and there are so many camera traps dotted around with poor signage and funneling with bus lanes that you can expect at least four tickets a year.

To add salt to the wound, they've started up with the LTNs (Low Traffic Neighbourhoods), which are so slyly marked that you can't tell you've entered a lion's den until it's too late. A lot of London's roads have been restricted to twenty miles an hour, which can almost send you to sleep. I like to look at architecture at twenty miles an hour.

After a good look at the art, I left and walked towards Victoria. It took me ten minutes to find my first pub, where I downed three pints. I asked where the closest bookies was and someone told me to go to Horseferry Road.

Instead of going directly to the bookies I found another pub along the way and had two more there, then I decided to try another place and had one there too, a total of six pints in under two hours. None had fruit machines.

Having rolled a little joint in the toilets of each pub and smoking between, I was high as a kite when I waltzed into the Coral. I thought I only had about thirty quid to blow (excluding ULEZ) so when I checked the bank app I was happily surprised to see that the refund of council tax from the last flat had been paid, meaning there was two hundred in the account.

To any well adjusted person, that would feel like good news but the fact remained that I needed to find four hundred quid by the next day to pay for the council tax in the new flat plus the week's rent plus the bastard blood sucking ULEZ shysters.

With a mixture of gung ho spirit and inebriation I placed a fifty quid bet on the nose of a firm favourite in a five-horse race. It came nowhere. Next was a fifty quid bet on the nose of another favourite but this one faltered at the first then refused to respond to a few whacks on the arse. It fell away from the pack and the other horses got on with the race. I tried a dog for twenty but it missed the break and kept last place throughout. I think it was looking for its owner in the crowd, knowing it would be beaten and starved for such a poor display.

I went to a digital machine and in under ten minutes the account was drained. I had twenty quid in the wallet and thirty-one pence in the bank so I went back to the pub to lick my wounds. It was busy by then, full of professional people. The workers' day was over and the services industry was letting off steam after being sat on their arses all day. The easy hours of early to mid-afternoon are my favourite for drinking in central London. None of this riff raff.

I went back on the tube and had a quick one at The Trinity, again making a fool of myself talking jibberish about the state of the world. On the way to the bus I got a sharwarma from the Lebanese place and wolfed it down in transit like a drunk idiot. Back at the flat I smoked a few joints and crashed on the sofa. Then I dragged myself to bed at midnight and at 5 I threw up the shawarma. After gorging on water I fell into a deep sleep.

I couldn't quite piece things together in the morning so I smoked a few joints and tried to recall events. I remembered being asked to leave one pub where I'd met and teased a stuffy old Tory pleb. The landlady told me I'd had enough.

At another pub I met a fellow gambler who tubed it in from Streatham to drink and gamble in Pimlico. He necked pints, hopping between the pub and the Coral, just like me. Recalling his face sent a shiver up my spine.

The more I remembered the less I wanted to think so I had a few more joints with coffee. Found in my pockets was the grand sum of four quid. With council tax, rent and the bloody ULEZ charge all requiring immediate payment I started wracking my brains trying to think of a way out. I'd asked one sister for one hundred and fifty pounds. This time I was faced with the gloomy prospect of having to ask another sister for a bigger sum.

I decided to wait to hear from the lady, who called up in the afternoon. I told her about yesterday, warts and all. She kept saying I need to seek help from a professional and the more she backed up her argument the clearer it became that I was screwed. There was nothing to eat in the flat and I started craving beans on toast, which my budget would stretch to at the local supermarket. We talked on and I pretty much caved in to her way of thinking. She said she'd be enabling me if she threw money at me so I decided to call my sister to see how the land lay there.

When I did, she told me that one of my other sisters' house sale had just fallen through and that her son-in-law was in hospital with a burst appendix. When finally the time presented itself for me to ask if she could loan me some money she gracefully declined. But then she reminded me about the money left to my daughters by Mum. I could, if I wanted to, borrow from that fund.

When Mum died seven years ago she left two thousand pounds to each of my daughters but because I have no contact with them I haven't been able to pass it on. I agreed at that time to lodge the money with big sis so that I couldn't get my greedy mitts on it.

In the end I asked for seven hundred and fifty quid and she said she'd transfer it. Once she'd done that I went to the Portuguese place but they'd stopped serving so I went to the supermarket and got myself a fish pie and some other provisions. Once home I called the lady and told her the good news. Then I paid the bills online and felt a heavy weight lift from my shoulders.

I met her in Victoria on Friday evening and we went for an Indian. She looked so beautiful I could hardly believe it, a more perfect face I couldn't imagine. I had two pints of lager and she had gin and tonic, then we went to a little pub for a quick drink. She is the epitome of kindness, as pure a human being as you could ever meet.

But she's also a married woman. And I'm a hopeless gambling drinker and smoker flying on the crest of a flotsam wave.

Yesterday being a Saturday, I got up and had coffee and hash. The lady called. She doesn't want me going out and gambling with the girls' money but I knew I would.

At The Prince Albert I necked a Peroni then went to The Beehive for a large bottle of Singha, which was crap. I looked online and saw a funny named horse running at Musselburgh so I went to the bookies and put twenty on it.

Returning to The Albert I necked two pints then went to the bookies on Electric Avenue. The horse had won but I drained the winnings in no time. Notes left the wallet and didn't go back in. The card reader wasn't working which meant I couldn't put any more bets on without going to the cashpoint so I had another pint then ate a ramen soup thing under the arches. I caught the bus up the hill and went home, had a joint, then went out to the cheap pub for a pint and double Amaretto chaser, then to the one down the road for a pint and a cheeky spliff in the garden, then to the bookies, back to the cheap one for same again, then back to the bookies and finally to the mini mart for a pint of milk. I'd lost one hundred and fifty on the day but crucially still had one hundred and fifty left in the account for the week. It wasn't the end of the world.

Kieran called up, having blown about the same down in Godalming. We agreed that we were just a pair of losers and left it at that.

The next week was ordinary but I did go to a survivalist supper on the Monday. As I'm back in London I got in contact with an old friend, Mary, who's big on dissent in the social media. I met her and her fella who runs a handyman service and when we left to go to the survivalist supper he showed me one of his bikes outside. It was the exact same thing I'd dreamt up as an alternative to having a car in London. It had two wheels at the front and one at the back. In front of the handlebars was a massive white box that carried all his equipment. The bike was battery-powered and went twenty-five mph. He'd ridden from Fulham to Brixton in twenty minutes, quicker than me in the car! I asked how much it cost but it's six grand a pop so that's out.

The survivalist supper was very strange. Mary hadn't told me what it was about, so when everyone went quiet after we'd been fed and someone asked, 'how shall we start?' I knew something was afoot.

A man with a deep, broad voice posed the question of what one might best do if and when the authorities turn off the electricity and water. No one offered a response and I was feeling quite punchy.

'Get the hell out of town,' I said.

'Where to?'

'A farm or a nice big estate, preferably a castle with a moat. Within two weeks of the cut-off, people will come looking for food and water. The supermarkets would have run dry by then.'

The place went quiet.

'The best bet would be to find a working farm and ask whether, in the event of it actually happening, you could go down there and work for board only. Or just pay the farmer to stay there. That way, when the zombies come a-crawling, you can fight them off as an army. A farm has machinery and tools. Maybe buy some shotguns too. Offer to lay some traps. That would impress the farmer. Otherwise, you could find some land, insert a huge plastic tub into the ground, fill it with water, then insert a metal storage locker next to it and fill it with provisions and a bit of entertainment. Adjoined to that, stick another interconnecting storage locker into the ground as a hideaway for the lucky few and camouflage the lot to avoid detection. Within two months, most people will have died so if you're still alive by then the world's your oyster. As you'd somehow survived, the authorities wouldn't kill you.'

One guy said he knew the people at Loftyford, a new age vegetable farmer, and another asked if he could tag along, half joking. I commented on how weird it was being there, sipping chardonnay in a zillion pound house in leafy Barnes, talking about how to survive an apocalypse. That went down like a sack of shit.

We left shortly afterwards in a taxi and I caught the tube back from Mary's stop at Baron's Court.

The host had been a very attractive little English thing, blonde, pert, tidy in all departments and an excellent cook to boot. As I got tipsy and mildly stoned I wouldn't bother to avert my eyes from her legs. She was a fine woman and didn't seem to mind my brash, shameless admiration. I think she knew I was only fooling around.

I worked the rest of the week apart from Friday, due to a particularly heavy night on the booze. Sometimes, when my emotional state is poor, the booze takes more of a toll on the old brain. Tony wasn't impressed but I got away with it.

It's Thursday of the week after now and I've got a day off so I'm tapping away and smoking grass and drinking coffee in the morning.

I saw the lady on the Tuesday just gone. We'd made an arrangement to meet but in the morning when she phoned I told her I wasn't feeling up to it. I was depressed and needed to be left alone. She got me round in the end though, pleaded. I couldn't say no because her heart's in the right place.

She came over in the car and I met her on a side street that's free after midday and only a five-minute walk from the flat. We came back after getting some soup and sandwich material, then chatted and played around on the sofa. By about two pm she was off so we walked down the hill to the car and said goodbye.

After that, I went to cash in an emergency support voucher that Lambeth had sent. It was for sixty quid to help pay for the surging cost of living.

When I did that at the post office I found three ten pound notes in my wallet as I placed the three twenties inside. I had no recollection of having any money at all so I started thinking how it got there. I've been smoking a bit more grass than normal so my short-term memory is shocking.

In Brixton I went to Superdrug and found an adaptor for my toothbrush. Plaque has been building with my poor diet and rather large alcohol intake and I've been lazy on the manual brush so the teeth have been taking a hiding. I'm too skint to see the hygienist.

To celebrate the purchase of the adaptor I went to The Beehive, had a cheap Punk IPA and texted the lady to ask if she'd put the three tenners in my wallet. She hadn't.

From there I went to cash in a small ticket at the bookies. I almost placed a bet but didn't, going straight back to the pub for another two.

I felt flighty after that. The flavour was on. The bus up the road led to the bookies where at the door the boys were hanging out. I asked if anyone had a tenner bag, my preferred amount because that way I'm only stoned for two days. If I smoke too much I end up doing absolutely nothing for days, which is actually quite constructive when I'm broke.

On of the boys said twenty so I agreed. Inside, I lost another forty quid on a few dogs and nags, then went to the cheap pub to make a nuisance of myself, smoking a quick joint on the way.

For some reason I was quite animated. I had two pints with Amaretto chasers and left in a flurry to get a ready made korma, doing the rice myself at home.

The money had dwindled to nothing in the space of a six-hour blowing session. There's so little money coming in that I see no value in it. Rent and bills paid, tick. But hardly anything left after gambling. The lady's upset that I can't go halves on a good lunch somewhere because I prefer to blow my money.

Actually, one thing I have noticed is that I do get the luck when I'm almost spent. If I've got hundreds or thousands, it's just a matter of time before I lose the lot but when I'm on the breadline I'm much more fickle about my selection. I'll scour the board for a winner when I've only got enough for a two pound each-way bet. When I'm good and loaded and well lit up I can stroll in there, see a silly name for a horse, laugh my head off and place two hundred on its hairy nostrils. Obviously, without research of any kind and acting on a ludicrous whim, the call isn't an informed one and the chances are well against me. I'm like a little boy that sees a strange piece of metal on the pavement. Convinced it's gold I go to grab it and proudly hold it up to my father, who takes it grudgingly then throws it away, laughing.

Apart from anger and resentment, the thing that loosens my hand for a gamble is alcohol. If I have three quick, steaming pints I'm down to the bookies like a shot, pen in one hand with ticket waiting in the other to be filled, eyes darting around the boards for a funny name. My mind addled, bets are badly prepared and found wanting so I hobble back to the pub to lick my wounds with the thing that lost my load. Alcohol! Feeding on that, falling deeper into delirium, I return to the bookies until all the money's gone.

It has to be said that I haven't had such a long losing run in years, not since the time I was going to Ireland to bet away the inheritance from my mum. That was five or six years ago and I was in a hell of a state. There was one horse when I was in Belfast. I saw it in the morning at the bookies and put fifty each-way on it, then spent the day drinking. It was an early evening race at Roscommon or somewhere and I'd almost forgotten about it when, drinking Guinness at Lavery's, I caught it storming home in first place. Grooving on down to the bookies next door I cashed in. Feeling flash I placed a quick bet on a wacky outsider in a virtual race and it won, another grand in the pocket and two grand up on the day. That was it after that. I ended up with a terrible throat infection and five grand down on the trip.

I went to Ireland three or four times before losing the lot. On one particularly jaunty journey to Ardara I went to a small fishing village called Killybegs on a bus for 'a day out' (out of the bookies). I walked around the place but found nothing of interest. The place was dead apart from one pub/hotel that served frozen fish and chips and one bookies that had reading glasses dotted around the place. I spent the whole day flitting between the pair, missing the last bus back to Ardara for another smelly lager and a go on the lucky last. In the end, someone at the bookies drove me back for my last fifty quid. I blew three grand that day.

This time round, in the last year, I've lost about twenty-five grand to gambling. That's a minimum. I earned every penny from honest hard work and then threw most of it down the toilet. The lady says I may as well have burnt it.

It's probably mostly due to the alcohol because that's what makes me bet by and large. Or is my fifty-year affair with gambling a foregone conclusion? Am I hardwired to bet?

The lady reckons I need a proper break from drinking, smoking and gambling but that's not an option so my mind is made, I'll go to the end. Or at least the beginning of the end and then get some help.

I'm a bloodclot on a blackout in a blizzard on the breadline.

I can sense my thoughts and feelings becoming more heavily tangled. They're almost at a point of destruction I can no longer withstand. It's happened twice before, when I couldn't carry on without help.

I went to treatment for alcohol and substance misuse aged thirty-two. Back then, it was all twelve step work with AA's Big

Book and I stayed clean and sober and without a bet for fifteen months. I needed that break big time but I went straight back to my old ways in a flash.

The next time was when I lost the children and became homeless aged forty-four. My mind had started to frazzle again and I needed help, holed up at the Wimbledon Y like a caged animal.

The treatment environment had changed by then. It was more CBT based with group therapy in the morning and one-to-ones every week or so. There was no insistence on going to AA meetings but I still went. Anything to get out of the house in the evenings. Breath test every morning. Going down the bookies was allowed.

Group therapy was helpful but I can't recall one of the counsellors saying that gambling was my main issue, even when they knew of my ridiculously sad history. To them, I was an alcoholic with a penchant for cannabis use. The gambling was an attached symptom. I stayed without a drink for three years and two months, without cannabis for two and a half years, but I gambled throughout. Admittedly, the reintroduction of cannabis paved the way for old behaviour but once I had a drink, the gambling escalated to previous levels in a flash and I was back on the merry go round.

Blair had just passed The Gambling Act, offering betting firms much more freedom, replacing the tobacco industry's previously huge advertising schemes for gambling's equally nefarious attractions. Firms laid their claim to the people's spare change and a casino world for the masses was born in the UK.

Gambling firms quickly moved offshore to avoid paying the taxes The Act was meant to claim back for its people. Throughout the nation, gamblers were being groomed and roundly ignored, just like in my day. Gambling, or gaming as they so quaintly put it, is now one of the mega-rich's hottest investment schemes. With gaming sites everywhere, it's boom time for the conmen. They're literally rinsing anyone, even children, within minutes and getting away with it. Tax-free too. Now there's a scandal!

In truth, though, I've got The Big Five; drink, drugs, gambling, sex and tobacco. I've been juggling them for the whole of my life and often wonder how I'm still alive.

*

It's Saturday morning and I did it again on Thursday. I can't do it for much longer.

I'd left my scarf at Mary's place last week (it took me a week to remember where it was) so I arranged to go and get it and take her out for a coffee but it didn't work out that way.

I walked down the hill at about midday, stoned from a morning's writing and lazing about. I needed food so I went and had a fry up at the café halfway down.

Making my order at the counter I saw two little girls at a table eating scrambled eggs on toast. Instantly, I thought of my girls and my heart sank for the thousandth time. Their mums were chatting at the next table.

It's far easier just to ignore children these days. A residue of pain has built inside me and there's a weight of loss that grows in their absence. In many ways I see less and less reason to carry on, a miniature wooden boat struggling in a choppy pond all of my own making.

At the start of my children's alienation I was resolute in getting on with things and staying sober, but when I fell off the wagon at about the time she carted them off to Berlin ten years ago everything went south.

There's no point in opening up with people about the situation because it always leaves me emptier than before. My own perception of people's inherent thoughts on such delicate matters is that they can't truly understand that which they haven't themselves experienced. The average mind just wanders off to what may have happened to cause the rift, inventing an unspoken fantasy from my reality. I'm sure they must quietly wonder what I may have done to deserve this living hell.

Walking into town, first stop was The Beehive. I had three there in quick succession. A woman ghosted around the tables trying to sell knocked off peanut butter out of a granny trolley but she was shown the red card. A young guy went from table to table asking for a pound. Desperate times.

A fart nearly came out as liquid so I waddled off to the bog, which was a smelly affair with no lock on the door. You have to carefully tease the loo roll out of a hole in a box without breaking the perforations.

I'd worked in the week so there was three hundred in the bank. I could easily pay the rent and have enough for the week ahead, even if no work materialized. But you know how it is.

Reasonably well oiled I trotted off to the bookies to claim another pathetic each-way win, six pounds. I had a few bets but nothing mad. To be honest I fancied a walk and a pint at The Trinity. I could roll a joint there.

I skirted away from the main road in an attempt to familiarize myself with the area and got lost within minutes. It was eerily quiet. With all the new restrictions on the roads and the cheap old cars out of the way with ULEZ, backstreets are now lifeless. I found a mechanic who gave me directions to The Trinity, right then left left left because everything had been cordoned off long ago.

When I got onto the main road I went to an electrical and furniture charity shop to see if they had a small undercounter fridge freezer. I found one that was about thirty years old. The white plastic had yellowed but it was quite clean inside. I asked to buy it for ten quid but the manager said seventy so I told him to fuck off. So appalled with his estimation of its value I even mumbled cunt as I left.

At The Trinity I complained of being treated like a mug at the charity shop but my protest fell on deaf ears. It was almost empty and the three staff members were looking at their phones from different edges of the bar. Realising that I should be gambling I necked my pint, rolled a joint in the toilet and then went for one more cheapo at The Beehive before bowling back in.

There was quite a crowd, pretty much all black apart from one lone white guy. He seemed to win on every race I placed tentative each-way bets on. He was vocal but without being too stupid.

I won on a couple of dogs and was about even when I put fifty on a silly named horse but that was a dud.

The white guy started chatting about something and invited me for a pint at The Beehive so I said yes. We went there and talked about gambling. He'd only caught the bug at twenty-nine and he was now fifty-seven. He asked me how long I'd been at it and I told him I started at seven. He didn't seem in the least bit surprised.

His dad had died a few years back and he was slowly frittering his part of the estate away. I had a pint with him and got myself a double Amaretto then said bye and went off to the other bookies on Electric Avenue, where I did another quick-fire fifty.

My eyes go a bit fuzzy on the sauce now and I'd mistakenly put 16 down as my horse in one of the races but it was an eight-horse race so the server told me it would go on the favourite instead. I had it each-way so when it came third I went to get my money but she said the favourite was a win-only option. I asked to see the manager and he came out and showed me to a massive board with minute writing. This board explained the rules of the house. I wasn't interested and told him it was a con, threw my ticket on the floor and waltzed out.

That was that so I went to The Albert and had two quick ones there. I was on the fruit machine when a drunk old boy started causing havoc. A fat old boy with a hearing aid went to hit him but as he swung at him he lost his footing and fell into a heap on the floor with the drunk just sat there on his stool trying to hide a smile. It was such a pathetic sight that the barman didn't even look over.

I went to the Lebanese place for a shawarma, then back to The Beehive for one.

Going past The Prince of Wales on the way home I saw it was open so I ducked in there.

It was pretty quiet. A DJ had just started playing hits and I was in the mood for dancing so I did my crazy moves alone on the floor and had a blast. I enjoy embarrassing myself. I know I'm a fool.

I think I walked up the hill but have no recollection. I must have gone straight to bed, completely drunk after an eleven-hour session.

The headache came at about four in the morning and I couldn't get back to sleep. If I took pain relief right then it could easily have backfired in an hour and I really didn't want to puke up again so I refrained until six-thirty. I managed my usual morning text to the lady and then I was out like a light.

I only drink spring water, even from the kettle, yet I'll throw lager and takeaways down my throat like there's no tomorrow. That said, tap water really is fools' gold.

I must have got up at three in the afternoon. The wind had blown hard all day with Storm Eunice ripping through London. I wanted some food but was too scared/lazy to go out so I ate some shredded wheat and a piece of toast.

The lady called on a walk and I told her to get back home. She took pictures of a fallen garden wall, a wonky tree clutching onto a streetlight and a flying dustbin. That day three people in the UK were killed by toppled trees and flying debris.

It's Saturday morning now. I'm trying to pick out a winning

combination for a football accumulator. Pretty pathetic. The Morning Line's on the box and they're talking highly of Saint Calvados, who's running at Ascot in the big race. The lady and I are texting silly love messages and I don't know what to do with the day. I've got grass and a warm flat so I'll probably just relax here. Maybe go out and place a few quid on an accumulator. You can win big on those.

The lady had a dream about me being found dead in my flat the other day. This is very sad. I told her I'd give her a set of keys so she can be the one to find me, which didn't go down too well.

I often wonder what it would be like to just not wake up. I've been thinking about that a lot lately. I don't go to bed praying it will or won't happen but some nights I quite relish the end. Overall I'm glad I'm not one of those people who are so protective of their mortality they actually cause themselves ill. No, I'm more afraid of life than I am death.

If I died tonight there'd certainly be a sense of peace. All my daily worries about money would be over. There'd be no more pain, no more lies, no more idiots, no more me.

I look at people limping about, staring into space. Then there's the news, all the barefaced lies that make up the most comfortably digestible form of truth tolerable. And look at the young! They've lost the fight already! They're as appalled by the future as I am but the only action they take is to scurry along to whichever corporation or start up will have them, where they learn to become the thing they most detest in the world; capitalism. Most kids hate it and rightly so.

Why should I care anyway? Nuclear war? Terrorism? How about a pandemic, just to get the party started? Then maybe a Russian invasion of Europe. And while we're at it, let's raise the price of gas thirteen hundred percent in a year. Make life so dull and unrewarding and despicable that death looks like the tempting option. It's a good time for zoom cremations. I've got one of their advertising jingles stuck in my head.

The worst thing about the current situation in the world is that my own daughters are growing up in this disgusting mess. But what can I do? What use am I? They don't even want to see me as far as I know. Maybe I've just plain given up, played into the bloated hands of the bookies, ready for the chop, a worthless piece of garbage.

Every day's just like the last, but funnier, stupider and worse again. My life is a stumbling walk through tragedy, a blind man, a bookmaker's feast, a riches to rags story repeated every Friday. The lady knows I'll never change, so why should she give everything up for me? It just doesn't make sense.

The thought of picking myself up and finding new purpose in life is vaguely interesting but I'm almost fifty-seven, a man putrefying. Besides, I don't think I've got another comeback in me. And I'll have been gambling for fifty years on my birthday so I want to be celebrating that!

The truth is, if and when the lady's gone, I'll have to start afresh on the love front. I could get away with doing another three years as a painter but if I don't change my ways and what I put in my gut I might not see that out without causing serious collateral damage. Being a painter is arduous and soul-destroying and all I'm really fit for at the end of the day is a few pints and a bath. It's not much of a life. All that dust.

I've been so broke I don't even have any proper gambling stories for you. I was paid four hundred by my sister for doing her hallway, stairs and landing but that got eaten up quick. I got a lump of extra strong hash on Friday night and I'm working my way through that.

Saturday would have normally been a gambling day but with only a hundred quid to my name and no work ahead apart from a kitchen job next Friday, I resigned myself to a measly tenner's worth of accumulator bets and then went into Brixton. I'd been smoking the hash all morning but still felt frisky. Having stayed out of the pubs for days the flavour was well and truly on.

First stop was The Ritzy for a pint of Hells out front. The lady texted that she could come and visit for a quick drink, then texted again to say the tube was closed because a young man had thrown himself onto the tracks. The overground would take an hour so that was out. We talked for a short while and wished each other a fine weekend. Not too much drinking, she asked.

I went to The Albert for two swift Peronis. The lady called again and went into a speech about how I'd never change and what that meant for her. She doesn't like me smoking dope, as you'd expect from a woman of her calibre. She wants me to be 'present', which is a reasonable request. We talked things through. Anything to get by and not hurt feelings.

After that I went to The Beehive for a pint of Punk, thinking I could go to the bookies down the road and see who was running in the big race.

As I got to the end of my pint I looked outside and saw a huge procession of very colourful people walking up towards Brixton Hill. I twigged that it was the march Mary had talked about on the phone the night before so I glugged the pint down and went on walkies with the marchers. There was a lady with a boom box on wheels so I stayed close to that and started doing my stupid shapes. Mary was there and I met some interesting people. After about a mile I ducked into a pub, got a pint and rolled a joint for the road up to Clapham Common, where the procession was ending.

By the time I got there I was lashed, a four pack of Stella from the supermarket under my arm. After a while the crowd dispersed and it was time to go. I walked back home zonked and stopped in at The Thistle for a pint. It was dead. The landlady was playing the fruit machine and there was an old couple at the bar so I moaned with them about the world and then got on my way again.

The next day, Sunday, was a washout. I felt about right in the morning but quickly got stoned and spent the day confused as to whether I was coming down with something or whether it was just the dope.

I've felt crap ever since, bunged up, ill. With no work on the horizon I need to make some calls and get the season going.

Tuesday started very badly. I can't say the fridge was empty because I haven't got one but there was nothing to eat and no milk so I grabbed a phone that an old customer gave me and went into Brixton to try and sell it. Trouble was, the battery was dead and I didn't have a charger so they couldn't test it.

Armed with a whole seven pounds I went to The Beehive and had a pint, mulling over whether to go to the bookies with the three and a half quid I had left. Then I had a thought. I could text my sister to see if she'd transfer forty quid. I did it and she sent it so I had another drink, then another.

At the bookies I won forty quid on a virtual horse then proceeded to lose, a few each-way nibbles the closest I came to a win. I had another pint at The Beehive, got a pie and some broccoli from hellhole Sainsbury's and then skipped the bus up the hill.

The pie was dreadful, dry and tasteless, five quid down the drain. I crashed out at 7pm in front of the box and woke up at midnight to hobble off to bed. There's absolutely nothing remotely interesting about my life right now. Satan whispers at the shoulder of the gambler, even when he's asleep.

It's Wednesday morning and the lady's coming over. I'm stoned and this will be the first time I've seen her out of it. She's in a stinking mood but has taken her dog for a walk which usually calms her down. It's 11am and I'm apprehensive as to how it'll go. I suggested she might take me out for a bite to eat in a text and she told me there was no such thing as a free lunch. I told her I'd had a joint and she was dismayed but let it go as a first. Best have a bath and spruce myself up a bit.

She was on good form. We met at Elm Park and walked down

99

to Brixton, ended up at a Japanese place in the market. We had to make sure they took cash for no paper trail and settled on no change given. Places still don't take cash and it's starting to bug me. Freedom Day was ages ago but a lot of the indie places have stuck to card only. Less leakage from staff, but it's not right.

We tried to get a coffee halfway up the hill but it was card only so we went to a little place opposite. She gave me twenty to pay and told me to keep the change. We had coffee and shared a cake.

Walking up the hill she again confided how her therapist had warned her not to enable me by throwing money at me. I told her I didn't need any from her, and that any normal woman would have walked away by now, but that only seemed to strengthen her resolve.

We kissed goodbye at the car and I went back to the flat to mope. Thursday was a haze of smoke and reading and telly watching.

In the night I had an awful dream that I'd lost my implant tooth on a cruise ship. I was aged about three and kept pulling at people's shirts to ask if they'd seen it. Nobody had.

Being Friday I got up early to get to the kitchen job in Epsom. The lady was nice and made me a frothy coffee. Miraculously, I finished at 1pm so I was home by two. Brassic and clucking for a pint, I texted Tony, who's in Mexico, and asked if he could pay me for the day. He replied that he would so I waited, looking at the bank app every hour or so. By six and with the Friday night flavour all over me I texted my sister to see if she'd transfer sixty quid and she was fine so I went down to Brixton.

The first pint at The Albert didn't go down too well. It's like that sometimes. When the old system isn't firing on all cylinders my tummy can take a strong disliking to the first of the booze. Food helps.

I was the only unaccompanied person in the place and felt very self-conscious. It's better in the afternoons, when the only people in pubs are diehard losers and challenged rogues like me. This lot were young and brash. They were also very noisy (when well adjusted young folk get drunk or tipsy their laughter can be utterly intolerable).

When I got to The Beehive there was a big queue, rammed with concertgoers tanking up on cheap drink, so I went to the bookies and played about for half an hour, neither winning or losing, just bounding about like a clueless toddler in a playground. That's what the bookies are; a poor man's stock market, or a poor man's livestock market, or a crèche for pathological gamblers. Horses are as much slaves to racing as I am but at least they get fed and watered. I don't even get bus fare home.

Back at The Beehive the concertgoers were gone so I had a beer and played the fruit machine by the toilets. I only had twenty quid to play with so I stuck that in and came out four quid up, which paid for the pint. I had a quick one at The Ritzy and then walked home disconsolately with beer sloshing around in my otherwise empty belly.

The only trouble with being an ardent outsider is age. Once you get to a certain age, you see how futile the concept of conformity is in the modern world. Then you carry on, without conforming, and learn how futile the concept of noncomformity is. You can't win. The human condition is no better or worse than bubbling, oily amoebae in a cesspool.

I thought painting was an honourable way of making a living so I did that. Ha! What a plonker! I thought that standing up for my beliefs would strengthen me but I'm a jibbering junkie wreck. I imagined I could make a difference but that went out the window years ago. I'm way too scared of authority now.

With age, the only real truth is the thing that sits most uncomfortably, that I've gambled away everything good in my life, even the kids. I've drunk and smoked all my life (apart from two spates of sobriety) and I've eluded every bit of love that came my way. Age tells it like it is and what age is telling me now is that these are the end days for my gambling. If I don't give it up it'll give me up.

The lady has a completely different outlook on life. Each day has to bring something different to the last and she'll do all in her power to make that happen. She wants to laugh and enjoy life, and no matter what's going on in the world she won't let it distract her, not even war. She wants to live forever, which is why she fears death so much.

I woke up this morning and started worrying about what would happen to all my things if I'm found dead in bed by the lady. Would she keep my writing? Look! It's in these two old laptops! I know I'm deluding myself to think she would. All my paintings and clothes would be dropped off at a charity shop. Most of the clothes had come from there anyway, dead man's clothes are cheaper. I recently received a letter from the charity shop that took in the paintings I didn't like and was pleased to find that they made seventy-four quid. Not bad considering they were the crap ones.

On Sunday the lady took me for lunch in Portobello and she asked me something.

'Out of ten, where would you say you are in your life at the moment?'

'Five,' I said.

'What does that five represent?'

'Having a roof over my head.'

'So you'd be at zero if you didn't have the flat?'

'Yes. Or maybe one for seeing you.'

She hid the terror of her thoughts in silence. Maybe she was thinking about my unsuitability and fighting it.

I just spoke to her on the phone and she wants me to go to Guildford to look for work. I've got half a tank of gas but the bloody ULEZ will set me back £12.50 just for setting foot in the car. I found out some interesting info about the tube. Apparently, the London Underground is the most polluted place in the city. Not only that, it holds the record as the most polluted underground transport system in the entire world. 160 years of soot and excrement. To put it mildly, the tube is a mobile gas chamber, bellowing invisible toxins from tunnel to platform. Levels of the most aggressive and cancerous particulate matter (PM2.5) were found to be up to ten times worse than on the roads. Air quality on the tube was recorded by the World Health Organisation as being five times over their safety limit. TfL use 60% diesel to generate its electricity so there's lots of nitrous oxide, not just the iron oxide (PM2.5) which comes from the friction of brake blocks and steel rail against steel track. It's a death trap down there BUT they're the company we pay to drive our cars on the roads! Nothing makes sense any more. Everything's the wrong way round. Upside down.

There's only two quid in the bank and no more than fifty pence in my jacket pocket. I've got some euros but they're in coins and no one takes them. Then there's the fives, twos and ones in the coffee jar but I can't be bothered to go to the supermarket and do the machine thing. It's too embarrassing.

I saw a job last night in Balham. It was a lead from a social media website that's affiliated with another social media website that won't let me unsubscribe. Much like a free bet at the bookies, this first lead was part of a promotion, just to get me hooked. After that, it worked a credit-based system in which you pay to contact customers who need work doing.

I swooped on the freebie. They were a nice couple and the job was to paint an outbuilding in the garden. Like a lot of places lately, it had been converted into an office.

Afterwards I went to a pub close to their house for three quick pints of Moretti, then walked back home. I hadn't driven so I was saving on that intolerable ULEZ.

If I call my sister and ask to borrow three hundred I can pay a week's rent and the overdue energy bill, but crucially I'll be able to have a flutter to see how my luck is. I haven't had a decent go of it for a few weeks and that's when lady luck usually rocks up. There's no work this week unless I find some today. Mary's boyfriend texted to say there's some painting work for me next week and the Balham job might come in but I have the rest of this week to get through. Food and drink will take care of eighty and the other eighty can be spent speculating on the gee gees.

You may think this is the very worst course of action to take now that I'm all but ruined but when there's so little to play with and without any real sense of purpose a little gamble is always in order, along with a few conciliatory pints.

The Balham job just came in so I'll have £650 next week. Spring is springing! The world is always a better place when winter is in retreat.

I borrowed three hundred from my sister and paid bills. After food and fags and other titbits there was almost nothing to gamble with so I settled on some pints and little ten-pound flutters on machines.

By Tuesday I was nigh on brassic so when I called the lady she insisted I go down to Guildford to look for work. I almost didn't, happy to waste the day reading Celine's masterpiece, *Journey to The End of The Night*, which I found drunk at Hatchard's on Piccadilly. You couldn't ask for a more depressing analysis of the human condition but I still managed to tear myself away from it.

I had half a tank of gas so I could easily get down there and back but then I remembered the oil, I hadn't put any in the old beast since November because of lack of funds. The terrifying price of it didn't help, a little plastic bottle that would barely touch the sides costs about twenty quid now.

I went straight to Wonersh Park and started giving out flyers, knocking on doors. Spring had sprung.

An old lady answered at one door and called to her husband

who came out. I was shown around work that needed doing to the exterior of the house and gave him a price. He asked me to put it in writing and his lady jotted down his email address on a piece of paper for me.

Then I went to see Paul and Diana, some old customers who'd turned into friends, or acquaintances. I hadn't expected to find work there so when Diana said I could paint the living room I was ecstatic. I gave them my price and they accepted so I asked if I could start Thursday with a view to finishing by Saturday lunchtime, another yes. I texted Arianne, an old customer who has a B and B in Godalming and gives me a good rate, but she was full. That meant I'd have to commute. The other B and B's are too expensive.

The lady came over on Wednesday and we enjoyed our time together. And then she was gone again. She's resuming with the therapist and her husband in a week and we both know what that means; silence and another long wait for resolution.

Work went well on Thursday and in the afternoon I asked Diana if she wanted a lodger for two days. When she asked who, I pointed a finger at my chest and she cottoned on. I insisted on knocking fifty quid off the bill.

She made a lovely supper and we talked into the night about the wonderfully colourful wickedness of the world, little stories of woe and whimsy.

The following day worked out well. I received a call from a lady in Godalming and went to see what she needed doing at about four-thirty. It was a ninety-pane window set with a door in the middle leading to the garden, a bitty job but a job nonetheless, to be internally painted. She accepted my price so I had a pair of pints at The Cricketers to celebrate.

Since a few years I'm usually absolutely pooped out after a day's work. A few beers gives me a burst of energy to get me home and flop. It's sad to say but now I know my job inside out I'm about ready for the slagheap. That would change if I got myself together but I just don't know how to do it any more. One drink and I'm back on the merry go round.

On Saturday, I finished the work and put the living room back together with Diana. En route home I went to finish off a job at an old customer's house and ripped a finger on a rose thorn. After it bled out the lady of the house put a plaster on and I finished off the work, then I got on my way back up to town and stopped off at St John's Hill for a pint and a flutter. I lost fifty quid on the machine at Churchill's. The din of the crowd raged with the tinny noise of the footy so I quickly sank a second and went across the road to the bookies. It was the evening racing at Kempton, where I usually lose, so I decided to side with the virtuals.

There was a virtual horse called Linger and Die, which I found very amusing, so I stuck a fiver each-way on that and it came in at 20/1, giving me the princely sum of one hundred and thirty pounds. After that my luck dried up on dogs and horses so I hobbled out about evens on the day. I got a pack of pork ribs from the supermarket and then went to another boozer I hadn't tried out, but it was an abysmal craft place, so I supped up quick and then stopped off at The Thistle to have a go on the machine, which paid me back what I put in. At home I ate and went to bed.

Today's Sunday. In my morning text I promised the lady I'd get the water hose for the washing machine and do a big wash but all I want to do is read, write, smoke and then go to the pub for the Arsenal match at four-thirty. A massive pile of clothes has built up since the move and I really need to get a handle on personal hygiene.

The boiler packed up a few days ago so someone's coming round to fix it. Energy prices are soaring thanks to the globalists so I generally turn everything off. I've got a system whereby I'll turn the boiler on in order to wash up and have a bath, then I'll turn it off again. There's something wrong with the central heating so I normally just huddle on the sofa in jumpers. It's not that bad but if I was with the lady, things would be different. Obviously. Deep down I just don't want to give my money to the energy shysters.

I'd say I'm clinically depressed. Thoughts of ending it all are becoming quite enticing (without being menacing). Whenever I speak to Kieran I can hear his concern. He's the only person that understands my relationship with gambling because he has the exact same relationship with it. We both worry we're going to top ourselves, which is one of the main reasons we keep in contact, to make sure we're still alive.

The Balham job's starting tomorrow. It's a piss easy job but I've got to walk there with my kit to save on parking and the fucking ULEZ.

I can't be bothered to get essentials. I ran out of shampoo, conditioner and other basics ages ago and I've started to enjoy living like a caveman, in a morbid but carefree sort of way. I only found my razors when I went to look for a new plaster in a kitchen drawer. They were hiding inside the plaster pack from when I moved two and a half months ago. I'd used the same razor for three months so a new one was a welcome addition to my bath. I'm using body wash as shampoo but I've got a good bar of soap, a present from the lady, which also acts as shaving lotion.

I suppose I could go to Poundland in Brixton before going to the pub and the idea of finally getting the water hose doesn't seem out of the question, but let's see. It's almost midday and I need food but if I go out this early I'll only end up getting pissed before the match. I've got just enough to pay the rent and buy the paints for tomorrow so I mustn't gamble too heavily, although I can always ask the customer for an advance once I get there. It's not unheard of in the trade so I can always fall back on that if things go wonky.

This has been my way for so long that every time the thought of suicide comes in, the less whimsical it seems. I'm too much of a coward to do it and whenever push comes to shove it's a completely different ballgame. The human spirit demands life.

I think it would traumatise the lady, and then there's the children to consider. It's a terrible thing to say but when I look at their faces in the photographs around my living room I struggle to accept that they haven't contacted me after all this time. What lies have they been fed? Perhaps, just perhaps, a dead dad is better than a distant dad. Maybe they'd have a better chance in life if I was gone and not just a living ghost. What frustrates me most is that we might never have a relationship. I should stay alive just for that.

What if they've been so saddled and weighed down by the poisonous, steely coercion of their mum that the venom has finally settled inside them, as if it was now a supreme tonic for their own survival as women? What if they end up never trusting men? How will they forge relationships when their minds have been so appallingly deceived? Will they go the other way and if they don't, will they choose an emotional wreck like me?

It's now Monday morning. A crow came to crow on top of the streetlamp just by my balcony so I went out and watched him with a joint. He was crowing at the building, to us. God knows what he was on about but it was good to see nature in action.

On his fine long black wings he hoofed it off to the next streetlamp and did the exact same thing to that block.

I went out at about one-thirty yesterday, straight to the bookies to go and get some skunk. I had a load of bets, almost all duds. The only vaguely significant winner was a virtual dog by the name of Scrappy Doo at 11/2.

Kieran kept calling. He was in a bookies in Guildford and he'd won his first two races. He'd won the day before too and was in fine spirits. He told me to back a horse in the next race. It was 6/1 in a six-horse affair. I didn't bother and it romped home. He then called to tell me about another horse and that romped home too.

I left about fifty quid down on the day, which was enough to have to ask for an advance from the customers, not such a bad thing. I can afford to get the paint but without a small advance of say one hundred and fifty I can't pay the rent, which is due today. So there we have it.

After getting a few bits at the supermarket next to the bookies I traipsed off to the Caribbean place for a suitably named jerk chicken takeaway. I stuffed that into my face at home and had a few small joints, then it was off to The Thistle to watch the match.

It was dead again. Just by the door to the garden sits the fruit machine. Above it, the large screen shows the football, but there's a constant glare from the hideous ornamental five-piece lighting block in the ceiling just next to it. Whichever way you look there are five white glowing blobs all over the pitch.

The landlady's a bit of a feisty one so you can't say anything. She's got those eyes that say I'll kick you out if you say one wrong word.

I fidgeted from one seat to another, unable to decide which glare was easiest on the eye. When I went for one barstool the landlady put her hand to it and told me it was hers.

Guinness followed Guinness and at half-time, one up, I went around to the other side of the bar to see if anyone wanted a game of pool. There were only two people there, one said yes so I set them up. He won the first game and we had another, for which he threw me a quid as he went to the bog. I think he won the second. The footy started up again so I watched that and chatted to the pair of them. The other guy was very proud of his dog, a ratter that could break a hundred rats' necks in a single night.

The guy I'd played asked if I wanted to take part in a pool tournament that was starting at six-thirty but I declined. If I did I'd drink too much, and at four pints in I was already on the way. There was a hundred pound pot which was tempting but I'm always too gung ho and fatalistic when I play pool, even if I'm on the black to win the pot. If I could just slow down I'd be a very capable pool player but bravado always gets me. I love snatching defeat from the jaws of victory. It's an everyday occurrence.

Kieran called again as the game was in its final throes. He was still drinking but sounded jolly, not the usual slurred rot when he's ten pints in and two hundred down. I asked if he'd gone back to the bookies and he said he only had ten quid left. I assumed he'd spunked it up against a wall on a dog in trap one but it turned out he'd fed his profits into his bank machine on the high street to keep it out of harm's way. It seems he really is learning how to play the game.

I wish I could say the same for myself. Every time I bet I lose so I should probably bet furthest away from my instincts, which are shot to pieces. Arsenal are playing Liverpool on Wednesday and I'll be paid up for the Balham job so I might stick a ton on something there. If Liverpool win they'll go within a point of leaders Man City. With only ten games left there's everything to play for, and it just so happens that I've got a ton on Liverpool to win the league at 4/1, a bet I placed back in late November. It's only a monkey back but it would come in handy to put towards an old petrol banger. Prices have gone through the roof because of the bloody ULEZ and all the other scams they've got going. We have ways of making you pay!

It's now Sunday morning. I'm sat on the sofa with a lovely cup of coffee and I got some more weed last night so I'm all set.

On Wednesday Arsenal lost to Liverpool. They're just too good, a nicely oiled winning machine. I didn't put anything on because I knew we'd lose, which would have been the best reason to stick it on the red shite, but it's not easy betting against the Arse.

The Balham job was laborious. It was so cold in that

outbuilding that the 'quick drying' eggshell needed to be left overnight to go off so I decided to leave at about one and go back in the morning for the second coat.

With about thirty quid to my name I went into Brixton. A quick text to my sister and she transferred a hundred from my girls' savings. I hate doing it but it's easy to normalise these things after a while. Needs must and all that jazz but the fact is I now owe fifteen hundred to my daughters, the daughters I haven't seen for nigh on thirteen years.

I spluttered around between the pub and the bookies in the rain but Cheltenham Festival provided nothing of substance. My right shoe had fallen apart and a squelch followed me around all day. After a crap pint of Hells at The Ritzy I dodged the fare up the road on the bus and went to the bookies. I got a tenner bag of weed and placed stupid little bets on silly named horses and dogs.

At home, I drank Amaretto and listened to the match on the radio, conking out on the sofa.

The next day I finished the Balham job and drove down to Wonersh to start the outdoor job I bagged last week.

They're a nice old couple. I'm using their ancient wooden ladders and it's hard work getting up to the fascias and soffits, cleaning off and scraping and sanding all the flakes and cracks to give a good surface for painting. It's my first outdoor job of the season and it has to be said that I'm enjoying the work immensely. The sun is set to shine for the next week.

It doesn't half take it out of you, though, and it just so happened that Kieran was about so I downed tools at two and picked him up outside The Sun. There's a traveller he doesn't like that goes to the bookies there so he gave me twenty quid to put on a horse running in the big race at Cheltenham. I put two pound fifty each-way on it as well.

When we got to The Cricketers, I was utterly parched. The first one went down in ten minutes so I got another. The money from the Balham job hadn't come in at that point so I was almost broke. We watched the race on the telly and our horse came nowhere. He got us another one then we went off again. I parked outside the B and B where I'd be staying and we scurried off to The Star for another two.

It was still only about six and I was well lit up so I took my leave and went back to Arianne's. Her son had just returned from New Zealand, where he'd been stuck for three years with everything that's going on. I went and got a Chinese takeaway and we ate at the table together. I think I held it together ok. The son recounted how his wife was sent back to Hong Kong for providing the wrong information on her passport. And she had to fork out for the extra journey back. Their young children are scarred for life from the experience.

Borders seem to be closing for one reason or another and it certainly feels a lot like war's calling its hand. It's been the same ever since Brexit. Maybe peace is the new war, fines and charges and price hikes the new bullets.

At nine I went up to the attic room and slept like a log.

Friday was much the same, a gruelling five and a half hour slog then straight down the pub, exhausted and in need of energy replacement. I played the fruit machine at Wetherspoons and sank three Punks, then I found some trainers at a charity shop. My work shoes had also fallen apart earlier in the day.

Arianne and her son would be spending the evening in town so I'd have the place to myself. I watched *The Irishman* with mixed nuts and olives but it was the same old Hollywood mafia drivel, the Italian/American dream regurgitated time and again under different guises, zillionaire movie stars slaves to mediocrity spewing out rubbish.

On Saturday morning I fried an egg, paid up for my two nights and then worked till about one. The old boy at the job offered to transfer five hundred into my account so I was ready to roll.

I had a couple of pints up the road and was surprised to see Tommy from the Bellfields Betfred. He'd taken the plunge and found a job as a labourer for a local builder. He looked happy and in shape and there was life in those young eyes.

I went out to the garden and got on the phone to the lady. We skirted around how things were at home and talked about general stuff.

When we finally got round to how things really were I felt like I was intruding on her personal life. The fact is, her house is a happy one with a strong and healthy emphasis on her children's wellbeing. There's very little friction in the house.

We both know that we won't be able to see each other for the foreseeable future. She keeps saying she can't not see me, that the thought is too much to bear.

I'm extremely unsettled at the moment. Drinking and gambling and smoking don't endear loved ones and the lady is right to be prudent. Either way, I can't go on like this. It's like having a girlfriend but not. She's a married woman and I'm starting to feel like the call up guy.

From the pub I went into Guildford to put in the cheque that Diana gave me for the work in her living room (I would have put it in on Wednesday had I not been so focussed on getting to the pub). After that I went to watch the tail end of the Arsenal match at Pews. We ended up grinding out a hard earned one-nil away win at Villa Park so I had a go on the fruit machine but not for long. It paid out six quid so that was my pint sorted.

Driving up to town was a drag. I got to Churchills at about four, had a few there then went to the bookies across the road, where I won three hundred on two virtual horses.

Stopping in at The Thistle was a bad move. It was dead as usual. The telly was blaring out bollocks above my head as I played the fruit machine so I asked if it could be turned down.

The landlady said if I didn't like it I could leave.

Horseracing was blaring out from somewhere else and the

news was blaring out of another telly. There was hardly anyone there. It felt like a madhouse.

By the time I'd stuffed thirty quid in the machine I was almost finished with the pint so I took my leave. Placing my glass at the bar I told the barman I wouldn't be coming back due to the rudeness of the landlady. As I opened the door I could hear him yelling at me to come back and explain myself but I kept on walking. He collared me outside and then four other people came out to quiet him down. He was rolling up his sleeves and telling me that if I didn't apologise to the landlady there'd be no tomorrow. I found this all quite amusing but had to keep cool. I stuffed my car key into my pocket so no one knew I was driving (they could easily have held me and called the police to breath test me). Eventually the barman calmed down and was led back in by his pals.

With the car parked opposite the pub I waited out of sight for a few minutes and then jumped in and drove off sharpish.

I've been angry of late, intolerant of things I know I can't change. There's so much crap and useless noise around and I'm picky about my pubs, but that's no excuse to be rude. Rudeness eats away at me, makes me ill with unrest. I have to keep a close eye on it. The lady situation isn't helping matters but I can't blame my mindset on that. If I look in the cold light of day, things aren't so bad. I actually won at the bookies for the first time in months and work's coming in thick and fast. Plus it's spring and the sun's shining.

On Sunday I relaxed with a roast chicken and stir-fry with garlic mushrooms. No pubs or bookies.

On Monday I got up early and drove down to Wonersh to get on with the house, arriving just after eight. I had a few joints on the way and felt wonky. It was horribly cold out. Putting my kit together in the garage I knelt uneasily as I threw the necessary tools into a dust sheet and gathered it up. With a pair of step ladders and my boom box I walked around to the back of the house and got going on the conservatory, which first needed washing down from gutter to sill. The old boy was sitting at the breakfast table inside as I drew hot water with a three-inch paint brush from a bucket on the steps, scrubbing away at the grime and cobwebs.

It was going fine until my lower back caved in. Working between the conservatory and a large hedge, the damp of the morning and the water-splashing had got inside me as I flung that brush around.

I could hardly get off the steps and when I tried to bend down my whole body felt like it was about to lock up for a spasm.

I made it to a chair at the patio table and tried to turn around to see if the old boy had noticed what was happening. The lady, who'd kindly filled the bucket with hot water for me only thirty minutes before, came out and asked what was the matter so I told her. I asked for some aspirin or ibuprofen and she brought some packets out so I gulped two down with a glass of water. I knew it would take about forty minutes to kick in so I waited there on the chair, my back straight against its back.

Every ten minutes I got up to see if I could bend down to switch off the music on the boom box but it was impossible. There was no improvement and each effort was as useless as the last. I saw the old lady grimace over her jigsaw puzzle in the living room.

A call to the osteopath proved useless as they were all in session. I thought about the lost days ahead, arthritis setting in to destroy any chance of work, the wasted days, the work I couldn't do, and then I thought about putting myself in the river and the cost of cremation saved. Then I wondered about whether they cremated for free once they fished you out of the water, although I'd much rather be entirely consumed by the river's living things.

After a while the pills started to work but any bending was still out of the question. The lady of the house, a nimble eighty-two, was happy to carry my equipment back to the garage. Her husband needed to go into hospital to have an injection in his eye so she saw him off and then came back. I felt like a complete idiot at my chair, watching her go back and forth to the garage with my kit.

All I had to do was walk to the car, get in and drive. Getting up, I found that the pills had taken good effect but any sharp movements were greeted with little shots of pain to the lower back. I went slowly around to the side of the house and as the car came into view I eyed it with suspicion. Could I even get in?

The lady said farewell and told me there was no need to worry on her part. I could come back when I was fit and ready.

Opening the door, I grabbed the steering wheel and eased myself into position with caution at every move. The road to Guildford was fine and my back seemed much better so when I went past my old barbershop there was no one in line so I parked up and had my hair cut. I got back to Brixton and had a long bath.

With the pills wearing off and still only lunchtime, I headed into Brixton to get some proper pain relief, knowing full well the real reason for my excursion.

At the pharmacy, the woman there served me the high strength ibuprofen and suggested eating beforehand so I told her I'd be having a liquid lunch down the pub.

At The Beehive I washed the pill down with a pint of Punk, then had two more playing three different fruit machines. The first two paid out small amounts but the third took a good hundred. It's not unusual to feel aggrieved when a machine doesn't play the game and a certain heady anger rose inside me. Smacking down a double Amaretto I wobbled carelessly to the bookies, where I lost five hundred quid in about two hours. I was a shitshow, really drunk and dazed from the whirl of losing one race after another, slaving away and then throwing it all away.

At about seven I went to the Lebanese place and had some food. About a month ago, one of the waiters there asked if I was local and when I told him I'd just moved into the area he gave me the fifteen percent locals' discount but the next time I went a different waiter said that the discount was only for those working in the area.

When I asked for the bill I mentioned the discount and this one gave me the new line so I asked to speak with the manager, who said he'd do it on this one occasion. I didn't take kindly to his tone and told him he could stick it up his arse. I paid up and left, shouting at the top of my voice as I got to the door, 'Cocksucker!'

Looking back, that's my ugliest trait. Not the gambling or the drinking or even the smoking. Anger has followed me around every step of the way. I know I was drunk and upset and I'd lost a monkey but that didn't warrant such complete and utter abuse. I'd like to apologise to the chap but I probably won't. I'll just let it slide with everything else in my life.

At home I felt like the most morose human being on the planet. The lady texted but I didn't answer. I got to thinking that I shouldn't see her tomorrow, that we should take time out for her to focus on her family. How could I even let myself or her believe that I could be anything but a walking disaster? I'd only ruin her.

If she was gone I could start afresh, alone but with no false illusions or silly expectations. I've waited three years for her but it's impossible. Her children have to come first, we always agreed that.

As a matter of course I best deal with problems alone and that's how I see my best chance of recovery from this hapless little life.

For the first time in ages I didn't wish the lady goodnight by text and slept on and off, knowing I'd upset her.

In the morning, as I was writing a text to suggest we call off today, she called and insisted on coming over. She was distraught and would hear only of my compliance to her wishes.

Looking around the flat I quickly tidied up the place. That's the only time I give it a spruce, not to please myself (which it always does) but to show her I'm still vaguely domesticated. Actually, I'm more nihilistic than I've ever been, a cranky caveman. She came over and we talked things through.

*

It's now a week or two after that, a Friday. I saw Kieran last Saturday to give him his ton and we went to the bookies together for the first time in ages. As you know, we hardly ever go together because as soon as one of us has a win, the other one gets the hump. Gambling is a very lonely affair, a table for one.

Over the last few weeks, even with his hand still playing up (lack of circulation), he's been in chipper form. He's taken the five thousand one hundred from the building society that he'd waited three months for and it's still sitting pretty on a debit card. I think he's playing that game to see if he can withstand blowing the lot with it in his possession. We all think we can outdo the monkey on the back. Some gamblers can, but most can't.

'It's a real game-changer, mate,' he said, writing out a slip in the bookies. 'If I'd put that money in the bank, it be gone by now. Easy.'

He's now deliberating on who to entrust the card to for safekeeping. It's a bit of a worry knowing that all it might take to relieve him of his hard earned money is a bad day and a load of beers.

While I keep losing he seems to have mustered a certain amount of control and it's been paying off in little bets. His van's been written off after an old lady smashed into the back of it last week but thankfully he's back at his mate's flat and he seems happy there this time. He's been living in his van on and off for the thick end of three years but not every night. He seems to have a lady in every village so there's always a crash pad for when it gets too cold or his cough's playing up.

Sandyman was in the big race. Reading from the internet at a bar, I had a feeling it would win so I told Kieran. Once back, he swiftly backed it at 9/1, fifty each-way. Rather than go along with him, I chose four outsiders at a tenner each-way a pop (Sandyman included) so when it romped home he was ecstatic and I was neither here or there. In the next race, he and I both plumped on Mowgli. Kieran stuck twenty each-way on but I forewent it, preferring a dog with a funny name at Sheffield.

I placed the bet for the dog just as the bell went so I asked the server if it had gone on. From his side of the till he could watch the race unfold and no doubt saw that my dog was leading. He told me the bet was too late and swiftly gave me back my twenty. I saw the dog had won and realised he'd probably taken my winnings of forty quid. Meanwhile, Mowgli romped home and Kieran was jumping up and down, shouting 'Go on my son!'

He's a generous gambler, though, and slid me a twenty to lump on another nag. He also tipped the server twenty from each of his wins, eighty quid up on the pair of us.

They're not all bad, though. A couple of years ago, I was so pissed that I threw an accumulator in the bin, thinking it had lost, and went home. When I trotted in the next morning, Kai the server was in high spirits. His eyes were popping out of his face.

'You won big last night, mate. Have a look in that bin and see if you can find the ticket.'

It wasn't the cleanest of bins, the liner still damp from the spittle of yesterday's losers. I waded in and eventually found it. Kai paid out fifteen hundred quid so I gave him a ton.

Kieran quickly waltzed out of the bookies with his winnings

in his fist and went to the bank to feed it into the machine, leaving enough for a few more bets and pints. The nag I had a bet on won at short odds.

When he came back he was dressed in a massive jumper. I asked him where his jacket was and he told me he left it at Gant, where he'd bought the two hundred quid jumper. This is one of the few happy gambler's traits, to treat yourself to something nice after a win bolsters self esteem. In truth, it'll just as easily go straight back to the bookies but it was good to see him beaming.

He was seven hundred up on the day and couldn't stop winning. Generous to a fault, he even slid me a little fifty win on trap one to cash in.

I spoke to him on several occasions during the ensuing week and he reported that he was on an even keel with the gambling, neither up nor down on the week. I was worried about the five thousand one hundred sloshing about in his account. Wasn't it just the devil laying in wait, feeding him with positive little outcomes to take the lot in one go?

'Put that card somewhere safe,' I told him.

He reckoned he had the perfect person to entrust it to and he'd give it to her the next day.

He called up today. He was in Guildford and reported an eighty quid loss on the day so far. He asked if he should have one more bet of twenty quid but there's not much you can say so I let him answer his own question. He hung up after saying he'd probably just go home but I knew he wouldn't. It was only half past one, probably three pints in.

He called back to say he was having one last bet on a nag at Catterick so I wished him luck. The call came and he'd lost so I asked him if that was enough for the day. He said yeah but I could tell he meant no so I told him to get rid of the card and he said he was meeting up with the entrusted person the next day to give it to her. He's still got eleven hundred in his normal account, mostly made up from winnings over the last week.

Ten minutes later he called back to say he'd put forty each-way on a Hannon horse running at Newcastle, then he called again to say it lost. A 50/1 shot won it and a 150/1 shot came second. He was going to bet on the winner, a Pam Sly horse, but he'd scoffed at the odds and gone safe with Hannon, which ended up stone last, the perfect storm for more catch up betting.

Worried that he'd start tucking into the card, I told him in no uncertain terms he was on very rocky ground. He agreed. Just before hanging up he said he'd put thirty on a dog and then get a taxi straight home to pick up the card, go back in the taxi and return the card to the building society for safekeeping, during which he'd have no access to it for another three months. I asked him to let me know when he'd done it.

'Get it done, Kieran,' I said. 'Even if it means you blow the grand in your normal account, at least the five one's safe. Look what I did with the six four the lady had tucked away for me. Gone.' He hung up and I'm now waiting for the call to say it's back at the building society.

I haven't been out today and I need to go to the bookies to cash in a bet I forgot about. I'll go there and I won't score any grass. I'll probably have a few low level flutters but nothing more than that.

*

It's now about a week later.

A few days ago, I went to the bookies and won a ton on my first race. Wanting a drink, with six hundred in the wallet, I went to the pub and played a machine but the longer I played it the more it played me. I must have had five pints and then went back to the bookies till closing at ten, by which time I was down to three hundred.

The lady was about to go off to Cuba with one of her daughters so we met at a pub in Chelsea and had lunch, then we had a little cuddle and she dropped me off at South Ken. I went to The Zetland for two pints before going across the road to the Coral. It was about four so there were a few races left. I won on the first and then went on a machine, which took up the next two hours.

After that I went back to The Zetland and met an American guy who was over for work and living up the road. He was an affable type, clearly proud of his three children, all grown up. I skirted around talk of my own as if it was second nature, deftly deflecting conversation back to him and his.

On the way to the tube I noticed a William Hill so I ducked in there. They had the football on and Chelsea were being stuffed at home by Real Madrid. An East European guy was the only other punter present, biting his nails, watching his bets go down the drain. He was playing two machines at two pound a go, his eyes flitting between screens. Those eyes were full of rage. There was an American race about to go but the server wanted to close up so I left.

On the tube I met a Chelsea fan and we got into a bit of a tussle but it was easily diffused. All I'd said was that it was the end of an era for Chelsea but perhaps I went a bit too far when I told him the dirty money had dried up for them, not that it's much different at Arsenal or any big premier league club. They're all foreign oligarchs' playthings and tax losses.

At Brixton station a guy tapped me on the shoulder, remembering me from The Golden Lion in Soho. He used to work there. So much for being invisible.

I had to have a pint of Guinness at The Trinity (they recently got rid of all their decent lagers and replaced them with local craft stuff, which doesn't agree with me.)

The next day, yesterday, I only had a hundred and fifty left from what had been six hundred a few days ago. When I walked into the bookies at about one, all I wanted to do was try and win a ton or so and then leave so I could do the same thing the next day but luck wasn't with me. It's Aintree week and by about two, my little each-way bets had neither dented or bulged the old wallet so I thought I'd give a digital machine a go. The first one paid out sixty quid from a twenty so I left that one and went onto the next machine, which paid out forty from fifteen.

At that time I wondered whether I should leave the machines and get back to the horses. The place was reasonably busy and there was a nice little buzz. The trouble with machines is that when you do well, you want to keep going.

Once you've played for a certain time, say ten minutes, your mind is locked into the game. You watch the reels go round to finally rest in one sequence or another, again and again. You know which combinations make money but, essentially, each turn of the wheel causes endorphins to flutter so a lose is as good as a win for the brain matter. As you'd expect, the reels usually rest on losing combinations. It's a form of mental masturbation.

On this particular game, the way to win big is to get three bonus symbols from any of the five reels. Each reel consists of a row of five.

When two bonus symbols appear, the remaining reels turn in slow motion to reveal whether the third will appear. It's a trick to lengthen the endorphin hit for the punter and thus fuel his desire for a good outcome, a double-edged sword. In general, when two bonus symbols appear, the third bonus symbol comes in once every eight or so chances. If it does come in, you can win anything from twenty to a hundred pounds or more from a 50p stake.

I scored a tenner bag of grass, probably knowing I was about to lose my load, then I went to machine number three. The first fifty quid went straight through, not even a sniff of a win. That's when you know the machine's a stinker but, crucially, resentment and pride step in at the same time, keeping you tied to it. You think it'll surely pay out but sometimes they just don't want to play the game and it becomes an exchange from which there can be no return. Conversely, the more you lose, the more you feel your investment must eventually pay off with a big win. Three bonus symbols will surely appear.

At times like this, I get to thinking that the machine has eye recognition fitted to see who's playing. If it's an old loser like me, they can be sure I'll be back so the machine goes on Scrooge Mode to rinse me quick. If the eye recognition doesn't recognise a punter, they might well let him win a load to get him hooked.

This is probably not a million miles from the truth, judging by the way things are going in terms of control. Track and trace is everywhere and the world's controllers of today are the very people that enjoy the rewards of gambling firms. It's vital for their gardening budget.

Paradoxically, and pathetically, I'd welcome eye recognition at bookies because if they all installed it at the counter and on machines and I'd chosen to self-exclude from all UK bookies, that would be the best way to confirm my exclusion and put me out on the street, which would save me the bother of constantly battling with my head's 'evil twin'. That's what the lady calls it.

Anyway, back to the bookies, a young lad was sat by the window playing a video on his phone and the noise was getting to me. Some people don't have the integrity of mind to understand the concept of private space in a public place. I could hear a young girl squealing and begging for mercy and the boy was laughing like a hyena so one of his mates went over to look. I was pretty sure it was a video nasty or very hard porn and felt contempt rising but what use would it be to confront them? They'd only have me beaten up.

By the time I got the three bonus symbols I was one-fifty down and only had another forty or fifty to play with. The bonus paid a measly twenty so I decided to go for another, which did eventually appear just before the death. That paid a paltry twenty-five, which went in minutes.

At the supermarket I got a fish pie, a pizza, some mushrooms, bacon, milk and a bottle of red to go along with the spliff. On my card was fifty quid, which went down to twenty-five so that's all I have left apart from a few bits of change.

Once I know I'm on a loser, slowly rinsed over the period of a few hours and with nothing more to bet, there's a strange sense of relief in knowing I won't be able to gamble afterwards. When I've got money that's all I want to do. Sure, there's work and seeing the lady and generally going out drinking but it's the gambling I crave most insatiably.

I won't wrestle with this loss. I'm so far gone I hardly care any more. It's just, 'where's the next load of money coming from?' and then I go again. I don't have any work apart from three days next week painting a bar and a bookcase in a swanky Battersea apartment and even that's not my own work so I can't be sure it'll even materialise. (Actually I just got a call and it's confirmed for Tuesday.)

All I've done for work this week is Monday and Tuesday, a quick job down in Guildford. Thinking I'd keep it out of harm's way I asked the customer to pay my earnings into my sister's account to repay some of the money I borrowed from my daughters' inheritance from my mum. I've still a good grand to pay on that but it's only April.

Fact is, I now need to ask her for a couple of hundred to pay for rent and food and roll ups. When a big job comes in, and it will, I'll be laughing. My oldest daughter was twenty years old two days ago and I haven't seen her for the last thirteen years.

I wrote a poem for the lady a few weeks ago. She went to lunch with a friend and asked her to read it from her phone. The friend cried her eyes out. Knowing that the lady hasn't been able to introduce me to anyone in her circle, she offered to meet me, which I found very touching.

This is the poem, just to show you what an old softy I am.

I often concern myself with why she loves me
but it's a pointless exercise
when a good woman's love is
as unwavering as a sparrow's
wing to its young.
When I look at her
breathe her
smell her
every atom is alive.

When I touch her in awestruck delight
and sneak a peek as I kiss her
and finally look at her showing all of my intent
she knows I love her with all my heart.

When I say the words I love you
she knows it's my absolute truth
and it's that truth that allows her
to accept her own love as truth.

It's she who I love
the happy lady in the street
the jolly friend always there
the vibrant lover flavoured to perfection
the fearsome mother who prefers yes to no.

But she's also a daughter of duty
and duly she is bound
to be torn.
When we meet it can feel like she is leaving
at the same time as she arrives.
Is it me or her

or is it just that time is so short
we rue the first moment as our last?

I often concern myself with why she loves me
but it's a pointless exercise
even when I have nothing to give her
but a broken heart
a battered back
a scattered brain
and a gentle soul.

It's now Saturday morning, Grand National Day. I just called my sister to ask for two-fifty, which will pay for rent and food and a few bets.

Kieran called about an hour ago to say he was on his way to put the five one back into the building society. I can't believe he hasn't done it yet but at least he hasn't spent it.

He called just a minute ago to say it's in. He's taken out five hundred so it's down to four thousand six hundred but it's safe now for another three months. He ordered all the materials he needs for a job starting next week and they're being delivered so that's another worry out of the way plus he's got a place to stay for two more weeks.

I'm not sure how to end this journal. In a way it's been feeding my gambling habit but I had to get it down.

I'm off to the bookies while the place is quiet to get some puff and look at The National's runners and riders to see if I can pluck a winner out of thin air. It's not even midday but I can feel the flavour coming on strong so I'll probably duck into The Beehive and get tanked up for the off.

Being so early the bookies was quiet, just a few old people staking a pound a go on virtual forecasts and wacky outsiders, swearing under their breath every three minutes.

One old boy questioned the amount paid out on one of his

paltry bets so he asked for a receipt. The server rolled his eyes and gave him his receipt, which confirmed the correct payment. The old boy just waddled off.

While this is a legally binding request, it's usually frowned upon by servers. I've known of a fair few quid being made on larger payouts from pissheads and unknown punters. In my view, a receipt should be given with every payout or at least a visible readout at the till.

There was racing at Newcastle, Thirsk and a whole host of other crap holes but the big day belonged to Aintree. I messed about with the early races, a pound each-way, then Kieran called up. He'd been in the pub since eleven so he was probably three pints in. He sounded very jolly, having put to rest the four six at the building society.

About a week ago he said he wasn't going to bet till The Guineas in a month's time. But he wanted to have a go today, he said, especially after putting away the four six, so he asked me to pick the winner in the three-thirty at Aintree (not the Grand National, which would take place at five-fifteen).

I told him to give me half an hour and hung up so I went to the wall and read up on the race. Some very classy owners and trainers were vying for a coveted prize. There were eight runners so the bet would be best attributed to an each-way outsider. Sire de Berlais was 25/1 so I plumped on him and texted Kieran. Then he called to say he'd put a tenner each-way on it.

A short while later he called to say he'd put a hundred on a nag in the two-twenty race, which was about to go. I watched the race and his horse romped home, leaving his rivals for dust, completely out of picture as he sauntered over the line.

Kieran had won three hundred so obviously he called to rub it in. When I say that I don't mean he actually called to rub it in, but when you're on a loser and someone rustles his feathers at you it grates like hell because you want to be in the same zone.

I'd paid the rent online earlier and bought a pouch of tobacco and a tenner bag of weed. All I had to play with for the day was a ton, which had risen to the princely sum of one hundred and fifteen quid so I was actually a little bit up. I'd also put a fiver each-way on two nags in The National and had a fiver accumulator on Arsenal and Chelsea winning.

The pub up the road beckoned. I smoked a joint in the garden with my first pint and then had another pint inside. The impact of my current state of mind mixed with quick beers and spliff sometimes puts me in a spin and this was one of those times. It's not a drunken spin, more of a whirling dervish, manic but centred.

The three-thirty race was about to start and they had a good big screen with a decent level of sound so I settled in, perched at a stool. I couldn't really hear which horse was which so I went up to the screen but it was no clearer with all the shouting going on.

Kieran called to say he'd put sixty on the nose of the second favourite, but as the race got underway he didn't look too well under the saddle. In stark contrast, Sire de Berlais was holding his own, quietly stalking the firm favourite. This pair had gone a good six lengths clear of the pack from the off and I knew I was onto something.

Turning the final corner the others were beaten, having their arses whipped to shreds in a bid to nick third place. Sire and the favourite pressed on but it was Sire's race.

As he passed the post I whooped quite loudly. He'd come in from twenty-fives to win at 16/1.

I strutted about like a peacock on cloud nine. Nothing can even touch that buzz. When it hits you're transfixed by a state of glory and wonderment.

And then it hit me. Had I actually placed a bet on Sire de Berlais at the bookies? I was sure I had, a fiver each-way at 25/1; a big win. I'd already totted it up in my head but I still couldn't remember placing the damn bet.

Ripping the wallet out from my jeans I delved into the slip pocket but the ticket wasn't there. I checked my back pockets and there was nothing, nor in my jacket pockets. I felt crucified, crushed and shamed by my own stupidity. Kieran called to say thanks for the tip and when he asked if I'd put it on too I had to tell him. He said my luck really was bad at the moment and maybe I should leave it alone for a while. I couldn't even answer.

I had another pint and a spliff out back, where I met a woman and a scaffolder. She had a puff on the joint and he offered us some coke. I don't do it any more so I said thanks and then had another couple inside.

My mind was reeling. I'd have to go back to the bookies and ask them to look at my previous bets. I was pretty certain I'd placed the bet on Sire at around two so they could easily find it, if it was there. Because of the amount of bets I place and my alcohol intake and general lack of wellness, my memory gets hazy and it's spreading quite drastically into other sections of my life. Even my knees are going when I bend down to do skirting boards. I have to click one of them back into place every time I raise myself up.

By the time I got back to the bookies it was nearly time for The National. I was steaming with five pints in under two hours. I hadn't eaten a thing all day.

I asked a server to look and see if I'd placed the Sire bet and was told it would take a while so I placed a couple more bets on two horses and walked away. When I reached for my roll ups in my pocket they were gone. I'd put the weed in there too so I was fuming. I looked around the place but there was nothing, then I went ahead and told everyone in there that I'd just lost a pack of tobacco.

No one came forward and I got to thinking they were taking the piss out of me, that they knew who'd swiped it or found it on the floor but weren't saying a word. I asked one of the boys for another tenner bag then I went to get another pouch of tobacco from next door. Back in there after a quick smoke I couldn't look anyone in the eye, enraged, confused, ashamed and inebriated. I asked about the Sire bet and the server told me I hadn't placed it. There was no ticket to be found.

I had two more shitty little loser bets and left a lonesome figure, friendless and desperately ill. Arsenal had lost to Brighton at home so even my little old accumulator was a washout.

I had a quick pint and spliff at the pub and then, with the last twenty in the wallet, I went to the curry house and ordered a meal for one. At the convenience store I got a large bottle of water and a pack of pistachios and then returned for the curry and went home.

I can't remember ever feeling as confused and lost and afraid as I was when I walked home. I'd displayed all manner of gambling madness in one disgraceful afternoon. I'd all but accused each of the boys in the bookies of theft, a terrible act of shame, and I can feel that I'm right at that point of no return. A fox came up behind me and bumped my takeaway bag with his tail as he went.

I can safely say I'm truly scared. I'm not scared of life. What I'm scared of is joining life as a non-gambling and drinking person in this increasingly ugly world.

Being a gambler is unnatural. It negates every quality and every feat of goodness that can be attributed to a person. In gambling I have wasted away to a shriveled up shell of a man. I haven't been able to recognize myself for a long while and it's time I got back into the groove of life. If I continue to gamble I won't survive.

I scoffed the curry and watched telly, flinging the shells of pistachios onto the coffee table, a drunk and angry oaf. The lady texted and I managed to send a goodnight text back and then crashed out on the sofa with the telly on as usual. It's a shit way to live.

Kieran just called to say he drifted back to the bookies on his way home and lost some of his winnings on a pair of dogs but apart from that he'd come away from the day unscathed.

Maybe it's time I stopped talking to him, just for a while till I get my head straight and fully working. Sometimes, just talking about horses is enough to get me back in there and I'm not entirely sure the urge will ever leave me. It's the purest form of delirium known to man, and with no need to ingest a thing.

Every gambler I've ever known has ended up on the scrapheap. From buoyant young pub landlord to reckless, destitute alcoholic/roulette player, master builder to local drunk/handyman/bookies bum/general hazard. It's a case of getting to sixty and winging it for as long as we can from there.

The lady's still in Cuba having a great time. I don't want her to read this but she's been asking to so I'll have to send her a copy. And probably never hear from her again.

Maybe this is a good time to sign off this jaunty journal.

*

It's now late August.

Four months ago I was well and truly done with life, writing and everything else. After my shocking behaviour on Grand National Day, writing it down was hard enough but reading it was horrible, like being forced to eat your own puke. I felt no prophetic catharsis, just an empty feeling that things would never change.

I went about editing the thing but the ending felt wrong, unresolved. I was still just a gambling drunk painter who hadn't seen his kids for thirteen years. Where was the story arc in that? Suspended in motion. A race with no outcome. A game with no winner. Another spree and wages down the drain, drinking on the low days.

Sometimes I'm woken up early in the morning by what I think is birdsong, but it's not that quaint. My own wheeze is waking me up. From about dawn I'm prone to cough up and spit about a dozen phlegm balls into toilet roll, throwing the paper blobs onto the floor. I tried quitting smoking a while back and by the eighth day of no fags the phlegm had completely dried up. I gained massive reserves of energy too. On the ninth day, something got my goat so I bought some roll ups and started up again. Pure madness.

I haven't tried my luck with publishers since 1993, when my first novel was roundly rejected by five or six of them. Back then, thinking I knew best, I printed and bound a run of 200 copies and sent it out like that, a real no no in the book world. It wasn't that good anyway but the process of seeking publication drained the crap out of me. The opening passage made it into an anthology by *Purple Prose* but then it fell off a cliff.

This time round, I didn't know the first thing about finding a publisher so I looked online and saw that all the big guns were accepting unsolicited manuscripts. Surely a good omen. They've been a closed book for an eternity and now they're all smiles and open for business? Too good to be true?

I called a few literary agencies to quiz receptionists and found that the process of submission was much the same between houses. It all seemed pretty straightforward, manageable, so I went at it but after about two weeks' hesitation I let it go. I just couldn't put the whole package together as an email.

Over the last couple of months, I've finally finished a novel that I started writing four years ago. It's about a young English guy who hitches to Rome in the eighties and stumbles across an underground cult.

It's a weird crime mystery with lots of twists and turns so when I couldn't work out the ending I shelved it. I'd written the thing in thirty-five days, each morning devoted to four or five hours' writing, usually with a spliff or three to accompany tea or coffee, then down to the pub and bookies. I'd got to the final chapter, even the final scene, but the main character still eluded me.

It's done to death now, with all the loose ends tied up pretty firmly. A few friends have read it. They think it should be aimed at the 15-30 year-old market. The lady thinks it's a bit lost between genres because it starts as a mystery and then turns into a kind of spoof.

Anyway, regarding getting this gambling journal published, I saw something on telly ages ago about a rehabilitation centre that weaned gamblers off their habit. I remembered the name of the place and it struck me that I may get a better reading of whether the journal had any legs if it resonated with fellow gamblers and their rehabilitation team. After all, they'd have heard it all before.

Admittedly, the journal is driven by the madness of gambling and with hardly a thought for the recovery aspect but there was no harm in trying my luck. Finding the number on the net I called the place up and spoke to a receptionist, explaining that I'd written a hideously honest gambling journal and asking if someone there might be interested in reading it. She recommended I send it to the CEO, so I did. That was late April.

After a few days, the CEO gave me a call. I was riding a tricycle through Earl's Court on my way to a job so I stopped and we talked for about twenty minutes. He'd scanned through the journal and found it, above all, extremely sad. Extremely anything sounded fine by me. We talked about how I went about my gambling with the alcohol as a sidekick, my past rehab experiences and the pot.

He asked how much I drank so I told him, around four/six pints on an outing but certainly not every day. Winter had only just left and I was still pretty skint, so this was true; the drinking was on and off, the gambling sporadic and often low-value.

As for grass, I reckoned I smoked a gram or two a week, if I had money.

In the end, he asked me a very simple question. 'So what do you want to get from this conversation?'

That stumped me. I thought of telling him straight, that if he liked the journal, maybe he could put me in touch with a reputable publisher that was hot on addiction and low life, but before I could answer he offered me a place at the clinic; a fourteen-week residential rehabilitation program.

I told him there was no way I could afford it (I'd just done a grand the day before, not that that would have touched the sides.)

Treatment was completely free, he said. They were a charity that found money from businesses and the state in order to help those with severe gambling problems.

This was an odd situation. I'd got to a place in my life, again, when I knew I needed to give everything up. Here, presented on a platter, was a way out, a way out of everyday life for a while, a way to reconfigure my brain towards sobriety and real life, a spell of self-imprisonment.

I was certainly grateful for the offer but my trust levels are shot to pieces so I immediately wondered what the catch was. If it was free, surely there'd be something fishy going on.

But this was the crazed gambling man thinking, telling me to carry on with the charade. The evil twin, the monkey on my back.

For a very long time, I've known that if I'm to give up gambling, the drink has to stop. It's a prerequisite to the cause, an absolutely essential form of abstinence that must be fully accepted if I'm to lead a gamble-free and therefore instantly rewarding life. With lager and gambling, my own Jekyll and Hyde story is on a weekly repeat.

When he asked if I'd like to go ahead with rehab, I coughed yes and he told me he'd have one of his team call me. They'd take things from there.

Four months on, I've been talking to the same guy, a pre-treatment therapist, every Thursday at 3pm. He's a nice chap but the sticking point (which has kept us at loggerheads and constantly thwarted my entry into the clinic) has been the alcohol and the spliff. I need to be free from those in order to enter mentally clear and present.

Initially, the therapist suggested I go to detox at another charity they work with and then onto a rehab place for alcohol and drug abuse for up to two months, but the thought of going through all those hoops just to enter the gambling clinic was too much to handle. Worst of all, the rehab place was in the same town I'd spent five years at boarding school, where my gambling took off in a big way.

When I was about eleven or twelve, my grandma died and left me two hundred quid, which was quite a lot in those days. Mum set me up a building society account and I quickly got into the habit of taking money out for the arcades of an afternoon. You'd have thought I ruled the world the way I left that building society. With enough wedge to feed those machines aplenty, I was in heaven.

Once I was tall enough to play the stand-up machines, my love affair with The Penny Falls died instantly. It was all about Space Invaders, Asteroid, pinball and, when I had enough cash, the new Nudgematic fruit machines.

These machines were revolutionary in the late seventies, a real money drainer but completely hypnotising. When the Nudgematic alarm rang out, you'd get five seconds to bring down a straight win. The jackpot was a fiver back then. Melons, I think. This was the most interactive gambling machine on the planet and I, aged twelve, was its servant and master.

When Nan's money dried up, I had to invent new ways to get it. I was only interested in machines, which meant I had to start stealing again. I'd done it since I was seven.

One very good way was nicking books from the school library. I'd squirrel them away and take them to the guy at the second hand shop in town, just by the tunnel that led to the pier. I got four quid for a bible, three for a dictionary and one or two for novels and suchlike. Other kids from school tried selling stuff to him but he only bought from me. I still can't work that one out.

The other way was much easier and almost risk-free. There was a farm shop in town that sold really good monkey nuts. After a few visits, the old couple that ran the place suggested I start up an account with them. This would then be settled at the end of each term by the school. Dad was working in Nigeria at the time and I knew my fees were being paid by his employer so I hatched a little plan.

I laid bare the plan to the old couple; if I bought an apple and a load of monkey nuts, would they let me have a fiver on top to go to the arcades with?

To my surprise, they didn't mind at all. I loved those two. They knew exactly what I was doing with the cash because I always told them. I visited every Wednesday (a half-day, free in the afternoons) without fail.

Both of these scams lasted a good two years but then my account at the farm shop was suddenly closed. At about the same time, the library started to plastic-wrap all the books with the school emblem stamped on the inside page. I must have been singularly responsible for this cautionary measure.

You might be surprised to know that I haven't stolen a thing for about thirty years but this was how I carried on in childhood, all to feed my gambling war chest. Going home for holidays was always tough because it meant I had to nick from Mum and whoever else was stupid enough to leave money around.

The pre-treatment therapist eventually climbed down from getting me to go to the rehab place by suggesting that, if I agreed to go to detox and only for observation, I could then enter the clinic. The more I thought about it, though, the less I wanted anything to do with detox.

The last time I got clean and sober was thirteen years ago. I went to a rehab place for alcohol and pot and they gave me medication for the first two weeks. I had to take a selection of pills, supervised like in *One Flew Over The Cuckoo's Nest*, but it didn't feel right at all. It was a dreadful place with dreadful people and by the time I was kicked out, after three weeks, a cist had developed on my right cheek. Holed up at my mum's, it grew into a seething, pulsating mass of pus about the size of a golf ball. It wouldn't stop getting bigger so I eventually popped it in a moment of rage. Watery pus flew out. It erupted again seven years later and they had to cut it out. It had eaten away a chunk of my right cheek muscles and I was pretty sure it was the medication that caused it.

All I knew was that I wanted nothing to do with medical intervention in a detox setting. If I was to have to go to detox, I'd go for observation, without medication of any sort and for only three days.

When this was agreed with my guy, he put me onto the detox people and I got a call from them. The lady on the line inferred that if I tested positive for cannabis (which takes at least 28 days to leave the system), I'd have to go to another place to detox off that. This put me off going to detox altogether so I then suggested to my guy that I do a home detox for a week but then he came back saying I'd only be able to enter the clinic via two options; go to detox for three days observation (er, no) or stay clean and sober for 28 days off my own bat.

If I chose the latter, I'd be tested on entry, probably by hair strand sample, which can tell which stimulants were used and when over a 28-day period. I knew all about hair strand sampling from my time with the Kafkaesque family courts.

If I tested negative I could enter. If not, I probably wouldn't even get bus fare home, but I could always drive to save a little face on the way out.

When I agreed to 28 days clean and sober, the therapist gave me an entry date, the 3rd of October. This means I'll have to give up the beer and pot from the 5th of September at the latest. That's where things stand now.

He's referred me to Lambeth drug and alcohol service and an appointment's been made for Tuesday to see if they can help me through the 28-day hell.

Two days before we struck the agreement, the lady gifted me a week's holiday in Crete. I'd started to look forward to that, my first real holiday in almost three years, and now I was faced with not being able to have a beer in the sun. It would certainly be no last hurrah.

I was due to fly out on the 8th of September and somehow, miraculously, stay sober. Because I've got a thing about taking my own laptop on holiday, I need to buy a mini laptop to take with me. I have to put this gambling lark to bed, screw the top on and never let it out again.

Work's been going well lately so I've got my head above water with bills. I even paid the lady back the money she lent me during the winter months. I still don't have a fridge and pretty much live on takeaways and pub food. I do have the odd red ruby grapefruit.

The supermarkets are so expensive now and the meat quality has taken a nosedive, especially in the poor areas. There's a good Somalian restaurant just down the road that does a very healthy chicken dish with rice and vegetables. They even throw in a banana and some salad.

I've had ants in the flat most of the summer so all food has to be eaten pronto with plates rinsed immediately. I hardly ever cook. There have been two heatwaves in the last month, absolutely crushing to the spirit and terrible for melting things. Butter lasts a couple of days at most, milk a day max.

About a month ago, the bastard ants found their way into some packaged sugar that I'd tried to hide up high in a cupboard.

When I saw things floating around in my tea I realised they'd infiltrated the pack and died there.

All the tops of bottled jams and honey, which I now sneakily use as sugar, need to be tightly fastened. I generally use Coffee Mate instead of milk because it goes off so quick in the stinking heat. Not only that, a pint of milk in Sainsburys has gone up from 56p last year to £1.05 so I won't buy it out of principle. The minimarts still only charge 69p a pint so it's obvious that the big boys are just milking the poor end of the market, booting up the prices here and there. The trouble with the minimart milk is that it goes off even quicker because of poor refrigeration. It's a tough old life.

*

Great news. I started a big job in Notting Hill yesterday. It's an Edwardian terraced house, three floors plus a basement. My task is to paint all woodwork, masonry and metalwork externally. The chap there's a lovely guy, very relaxed in that urban upper-class way.

With Summer Bank Holiday this weekend, the buzz is building around the place. Carnival starts on Sunday.

I started the job on Friday, got there at half seven, the drive from Brixton only thirty minutes now everyone's on holiday. Parking on a meter outside the house the gent opened the door and I piled all my kit in. There was a little area in the garden for storing everything.

I got stuck in, raking and hacking out rot from a massive window set at back of house. The putties had blown in areas and the sills and window joints needed attention but they weren't in terrible condition. Very manageable, but lots of it. The parking bay limit's four hours were up so I found a different spot for two hours, rolled a spliff and smoked it on the way to the pub.

The barman didn't like it when I asked for less froth and then he tried to charge me service from the bar when I ordered some tapas. The manager intervened and the barman stormed off. The manager then told me that the barman had just that morning discovered he has a heart condition.

I felt awful but there we are. He came back and I apologised, we made up. I did another hour or so at work then gave up.

The drive home was interrupted when I stopped off at The Churchill on Ken Church Street, parking on a meter for ninety minutes.

I got chatting to two Americans, a retired gentleman from Houston and a thickset, intense guy from Long Island. I had two there (the Houston man buying one), then trotted off to William Hill to place a bet on the 4.10 at Thirsk.

It was a nine-horse race and I fancied a few names so I put a tenner each-way on three of them, then it was off to The Old Swan next door for a pint and a go on the fruit machine. I won or lost a little then looked at the time and saw that the meter had expired so I went back to the car without seeing how the bet had gone at the bookies.

As I was driving along Gloucester Road the thought of another pint seemed perfectly reasonable so I stopped off at The Hereford and met a funny Japanese guy and his young friend from Persia. I'd parked in a resident's bay just opposite so I didn't stay long.

The drive back was arduous but manageable, with Public Enemy's *Fear of a Black Planet* belting out of the speakers. I don't listen to anything else in the car. It's perfect for London traffic, pure meaty, angry adrenaline.

I got an Indian takeaway and crashed out on the sofa.

The day before, I'd gone into Soho early doors for a jaunt and forgotten to eat so the lager really did its thing. I had three or four at The Golden Lion, where they'd changed the fruit machine. I played the new one and won about thirty quid, then chatted to the barmaid. She wants to be a songwriter but spends fourteen hours a day serving pints to deadheads like me.

It was nice and quiet and an old boy came in, ordered a double scotch (at just past midday) and then used the bottled sanitiser on the bar to wash his hands.

'Wow, you order scotch and then wipe your hands with that crap?'

He took it with a pinch of salt, but the world's undoubtedly gone mad.

My luck at the bookies in Chinatown was appalling, losing a monkey overall. I switched from Paddy Power to the Betfred mid-afternoon, seeing as it was just next to O'Neills, where I took intermittent sherbets and goes on the old school fruit machine, chatting to strangers outside with a fag, in between bouts back at the bookies next door. Not one virtual horse placed and all my nags came last or second last.

I had a Korean meal somewhere but it was crap so I got the tube back home and didn't even have the strength to go to The Ritzy for one last beer.

One of my horses at the Thirsk race won at 17/2 so there's one-twenty coming back from that, a sixty quid profit.

As you can see, things haven't exactly changed. I'm still the gambling and drinking nutcase.

I saw a medium for the first time last Wednesday and he told me that I was being looked after by what he thought was my grandfather, or someone from my father's side, and also by my mother, who was always by my side. He showed me where she was, there in his living room, immediately to my left, just in front of the telly. You'd love my mum, she's the kindest person in the world. The someone from my father's side was to the right of and behind the medium, which, according to him, was most unusual.

During the mediumship, he discovered from spirits that

I would come into a load of money for a work project of some kind. The future was very bright. The windfall would take place almost directly after my holiday. This would, he insisted, be a time for transformation and renewal.

I wanted to think that the amazing thing would be one of the books getting snapped up and turned into a film and me becoming a big restaurant critic for the papers, but it was probably all about rehab.

Tarot was the second part of the session so he casually shuffled a pack of cards and then splayed them face down across the table between us, asking me to pick out fourteen cards from anywhere.

I chose a clump to my middle-right of the pack and picked it up, counting to exactly fourteen and passing them to him.

His face was a picture. 'In eighteen years of doing this, I've never seen anyone pick out fourteen cards like that.'

As he laid the cards down before me, it again became clear that I'd come into loads of money. I explained that this would be highly unusual, outside of winning the lottery, but he was having none of it. I would be very comfortable, he insisted.

The cards also confirmed that my mother and the someone on my dad's side indeed were/are there/here with me, and that they always would be. The medium even got one or two clouts from what he thought was my grampa.

I've since wondered whether the someone from my father's side is actually A S Jasper, my great uncle, with whom I already have previous afterlife experience. Or maybe it's his dad, the feckless alcoholic father.

I say I have previous afterlife experience with A S Jasper because, about twelve years ago, I attended a writers' group in Putney and received a visit from him. Once a month, eight of us would meet at a house and read passages of work around a dining table. The average age was about seventy.

Sometimes, I'd lose interest and my eyes would wander off to a certain book at the top of a large bookcase. It was a hardback from the late sixties, the spine's purple psychedelic lettering in large format.

For about a year, I took comfort from that spine, just looking at it, my kind of lettering. Then my sister called me up to say that there's a writer in the family. I asked who it was and before she told me, I KNEW she'd say A S Jasper. It was the weirdest but also the most convincing thought I've ever had, and it turned out to be right. It was indeed A S Jasper, and it was his book, *A Hoxton Childhood*, that had winked at me at the writers' group.

Back to the cards, on the love front, I had the four of hearts, which meant that the lady isn't yet ready to commit herself, which is indeed the current situation, mostly due to my appalling ways. Above all, she has her family to consider and her children must come first, as has always been the case.

There also, smack in the middle of my pack, was The World. The medium said I'd be doing a whole load of travelling in future.

Directly below this card was Temperance, and I knew that all I had to do to get to my dream was be clean and sober and without a gamble, preferably for about three years. Just get to sixty and see what happens.

To confirm my projected windfall, I had the three, five and queen of Gems.

Now, with temperance surely on its way, completing the journal seems the best option. It can be my last chance to relay the dark, bouncy, crazy, sad side of life; the turmoil of gambling and drinking as a lonesome middle-aged man.

I've been enjoying my little jaunts to various pubs and, to a lesser extent, even the bookies. I don't feel chained to gambling like before, but maybe that's because I've got work, hence why the pubs are more enjoyable, away from Brixton and back in my favourite area, Notting Hill. I'm still losing big time, though.

Nothing's changed there.

With work being so full on, the drinking's gone up a couple of notches, plus I've been going at the puff, hence why I haven't found the time to write. I've put bullet points into Notes on the phone so it's all there to be set down in the goodness of time.

If I can stay clean and sober from the 5th of September, which is nine days away, I'll enter a treatment program specifically designed to manage my gambling affliction for the very first time. This is my fiftieth year of pathological gambling so it's high time.

The lady's on holiday with her family but we'll see each other when she gets back and then I'm heading off for my alcohol-free holiday. She dreads me going away to rehab for fourteen weeks but she wants me to do it. She's been a real rock.

This job's worth six grand so I'll be able to buy a half decent petrol banger *and* pay a grand or two back to my daughters' account with my sister, which I've almost depleted.

These next nine days will be a homage and goodbye to drinking and smoking dope and gambling. Thereafter, I'll be working for another three weeks on the Notting Hill job with Crete in the middle. That's my 28 days.

Apparently, when you enter rehab, you effectively go on the dole so rent and council tax are taken care of, which is a real bonus. I'll be spending Christmas there but that's no bother. I just want freedom from gambling and drinking so I can make something of myself.

The medium told me I'd do something connected to corruption so I told him about my dream of winning the lottery and setting up a whistle-blowing company to expose scammers. Living as I do, you'll think I'm a real hypocrite but I'm not that bad. The only person I scam is me.

Anyway, the world's my oyster if the cards are to be believed. It's funny but when I picked up that clump from the splayed deck I knew there'd be fourteen. I'd had a bet with myself as

I did it!

It's free parking in Notting Hill on Saturday afternoons but I still have to pay the bastard ULEZ.

I got to the job just after ten and put the car on a meter for three hours. The customer was visiting relatives in the country so I let myself in, turned off the alarm and got going, scraping off flaky paint from the front railings. By 3pm I'd had enough so I went to the pub and offered to buy the barman a drink but he declined.

With carnival starting next day there was a good buzz around Portobello so I had two there and then went for a quick one at The Elgin, then on to the bookies across the road. (The Coral, which is visible from the house, seems to have closed down.)

Arsenal were playing Fulham in the late kick-off so I went back to The Elgin to watch a bit of that. The Gunners were playing well but the Cottagers were dogged in defence. At half-time it was still nil-nil so I went back to the bookies and put something on over 2.5 goals and over 3.5 goals, knowing it could be a rout in the making.

In the end, we won 2-1 so I got a bit back but I lost the lion's share of a monkey overall.

I needed to pick up my winnings from the Thirsk race so I drove up to Notting Hill Gate and parked by The Churchill, where I took a sharpener before bowling into William Hill.

Bungley, the horse, paid out one-twenty so I started playing Centurion on a machine. At two pound a spin, a tenner can go in under ten seconds on AutoPlay.

It was nearly ten o'clock and an announcement was made by tannoy that the shop would close in five minutes. Anyone playing a machine should cash in their winnings. As I only had about forty quid in mine I played on and, right at the death, Caesar gave me fifty free spins so I shouted just that. 'I got fifty free spins!'

The only people in the place were me and the server, who was on the phone. When I looked back at the machine it had only registered five free spins, which paid out a paltry eight quid.

'It just did me out of forty-five free spins!' I shouted at her. 'Can you ask the guy on the phone to look into it?'

She said there was nothing to be done and I was furious, not at her but at the bastards who'd just diddled me out of anything from fifty to two hundred quid. I got to thinking there was facial recognition built into the machine and that some arsehole bookie wanker in Gibraltar (probably the guy on the phone) was watching me and taking the mickey.

As my funds dwindled to nothing, I spoke to the machine, thinking he was listening. 'You greedy, mindless little termite. Go fuck your mum in the mouth, you brown-nose cunt.' I know it's terrible, heinous language but losing makes me so mad.

There was nothing I could do but walk away. They probably had CCTV ready for any exploits, just waiting for me to blow my top and get the filth in to take me away with an ITV film crew, but you won't catch me playing their silly games. I left without fuss.

A consolatory pint at The Churchill took the edge off but I was livid, once again shafted by myself. I went back home but I wasn't done there so I had a spliff and wandered down to the cheap pub (that I haven't been to for about four months) for a dance. I met an attractive Dutch woman at the bar and a load of young guns started shoving me about as I talked to her. It was surreal, barge after barge and we just kept on talking. All they needed was a reaction and I'd be laid out cold. Yet more silly games.

Apparently, I reminded her of her favourite person in the world, an uncle. She spun me around and around on the dancefloor and then we went outside to talk to her mates. One was a German woman. She was pissed and asked me where I was from so I told her I was English.

'Ha! You're the minority! You know that, don't you?' she

said, poking a finger at my chest.

I didn't want to make anything out of it so I said bye to the Dutch woman and trotted off.

I got up at seven the next day, Sunday, to get into work well before the carnival crush. The drive was sumptuous, hardly a soul around, and I made it up there in twenty minutes, a minor miracle.

After a bit of work I went out and got a cappuccino and a ham and cheese croissant. Walking down Portobello, I passed by a house I'd visited with a friend about thirty-five years ago. It had belonged to one of her friends from convent school and she'd just come back from Epsom, where she'd won four grand. According to her, she was one of a select little group of people that knew the outcome of at least two races at every meeting they went to.

For some reason, the thought of this tawdry lot having real inside knowledge sickened me and I told her she was bent. She took offence and I was asked to leave. It was an insignificant shitshow.

I got back to prep windows till about one and then went out again to sample the atmosphere. It was still building, easy enough to move about. I had a jerk chicken box in Powis Square and perched on a bike-rental block to eat up. The pub was open so I had a couple there and returned for an afternoon stint on the windows.

At five I'd had it so I went back to the pub and bumped into a chap I met at The Antelope in Belgravia about two months ago. He's a guitarist and on the night we met, he walked in at last orders and asked for a pint of Peroni and a double Jack. I was so impressed I spent the last of my money on a Peroni and a double Amaretto. We got talking and exchanged numbers with a drunken view to working on a song together.

I had a couple of beers with him and then got on my way. Dressed in my painting gear (cut jean shorts and paint-spattered t-shirt, quite clean khaki Camel jacket with socks and slip-on Skechers) I was whacked out from working tight angles on the back windows in the baking sun. With a few spliffs too.

Every street was heaving, a massive wall of people stretching forever with sound systems booming out beats at fifty-yard intervals. Wading through the thick mass of bodies I got to the Gaz's Rockin' Blues stage and rolled a quick joint with the last of the grass, then I turned a corner and there was a big black guy selling weed out of a supermarket bag. I inspected it with a sniff and he wanted a tenner for a good pinch. Two American girls of about twenty said they only wanted enough for a joint so I suggested we go halves. In the end they bought it and I rolled us a big one. A group of police officers walked by nonchalantly with the big guy holding out his bag to passersby. Hilarious!

We sat at the curb to smoke the joint and one of the girls asked me to tell her something about myself so I relayed the time I went to carnival on acid at about their age.

Here's the crack; I was high on acid, taking a piss down a mews when a pair of police officers told me to stop what I was doing so I held it in mid-slash and did my zip up. When they let me go, I waded into the crowd on All Saints Road and then turned around, flicking v-signs at them. They raced in and got me, then dragged me down the length of the mews to an area completely cordoned off from the public. There was a massive coach with dozens of coppers having tea at its undercarriage. It was quite surreal. I was asked to explain myself to the cop in charge and told him what I'd done. He looked at the two coppers.

'Well,' he said, 'he's one of us so what do you reckon?' This was insinuating that, because I was white, they'd let me go.

'If you're letting me go because I'm white you may as well take me in,' I said.

And that was that. I was taken in alright, straight off in a white van and driven to another part of the carnival (they drove through the crowds in those days). When I got there I was placed in a cubicle on a specially designed coach and left to stew for four hours. Then, for whatever reason, they took me down to Scotland Yard, where I was again placed in a cell. After a few hours, with the acid wearing off, I was released.

'Your mother says you've been a very naughty boy,' the cop on duty said. 'You can go now.'

Already well into the evening and with no money to go anywhere, I dipped into a pub, told my story to a bloke and he gave me enough for a bus ride back to carnival, but it had ended for the day. I was living around there so I just went home.

I think the girls were already a bit pissed but the joint had a terrible effect on one of them. She'd rammed her whole fist into her mouth and was retching quietly to herself. I told her she needed to stop. She looked at me mournfully. God knows what was going on in her head.

We got up from the pavement and she dropped her phone so I picked it up, gave it back to her and told the other girl to look after her. The arse of her white jean shorts was covered in wet street dirt.

Watching them leave got me thinking about my own daughters, who are now of the age to go a bit wild. I prayed they're alright. They could have been there, at carnival, experimenting. I'd never know. I don't even know what they look like.

I got to The Old Swan at the Gate but they were only doing pints in plastic cups so it was off to The Churchill to have it in a glass there.

The drive home was again an absolute piece of piss, a half-hour at most. I got a takeaway at the Caribbean place, scoffed it down and crashed on the sofa with the telly on as usual. August is the best month to drive in London. All the well off are well off somewhere nice and hot and beachy.

The next day, Bank Holiday Monday, I drove to work in a

happy state of mind and again parked up on a side street off Ken Church Street. It was the second and last day of carnival.

I did a load of work till two then went and had a few beers, returning to undercoat a load of sash windows at the back. Knocking off at five I went back to the pub to find the guitarist and his buddy looking worse for wear. They'd been up till 4am the night before, the poor devils.

Wading through the crowds to get out, police presence was enormous, marching sometimes three deep in wide processions.

Stopping off at a pub up behind The Gate I had one there. A young guy said 'hello, grandad' and I suddenly realised that my age was starting to show, what with everything I've been doing. I went to Hills for a gamble but they were about to close early so I went to The Churchill for a pint and a Pad Thai.

Waiting for my food, there were three couples at little tables dotted around. They all stared at their phones for a good five minutes. Not a word passed between these young and otherwise attractive people.

If the road home yesterday was a piece of piss, this evening was a whole streak of it. I don't think I hit one red light the whole way, arriving back in a paltry twenty minutes. There was one incident on Gloucester Road, an Audi TT driven by a nutcase, swerving into a crossing female pedestrian at the intersection with Cromwell Road.

He just missed her. I let the woman pass but then the Audi backed into a spot and almost sideswiped me. He was about twenty, being goaded on by an even stupider friend. Too much money.

It's Tuesday morning and I just got back from Lambeth drug and alcohol service. When I arrived at the appointment time, quarter to nine, the security guy was standing outside. He said it opened at nine so I told him about the appointment time and he said that was unusual but I'd still have to wait.

I wanted to get this over with as quickly as possible so I could get on with my day. I thought of just leaving, taking the tube to work and telling my guy at the gambling clinic that I didn't have time to wait.

Having just eaten a chicken bake from Greggs with a cappuccino my bowels weren't happy and I needed the loo. The security guy let me in through a side door and waited in the corridor for me. I teased out enough paper from the impossible roll-pulling box to wipe down the seat and it went flying. I tried to catch it and that's when my lower back went. I knew I was in trouble.

It's most prone to go when I'm angry and lacking in humility, and especially when I'm working at tight angles, which I had been for the past few days. There's a knack to working on the exterior of a large sash window set from the inside. You sit yourself down on the masonry of the sill and scrape from there. Then you stand up and balance yourself while scraping, sanding and filling the high areas. Everything goes in your face but you learn to breathe sparingly when debris and dust are around.

Leaving the loo, I heaved the door open and the security guy thought I was done so I told him the seat was fucked and that I needed to use the disabled loo instead. I had my crap and was returned outside, where a little mob of users had gathered. It turned out that it's first come, first served so when we went in at nine I was seen by the receptionist and given a form to fill in. Someone would be along shortly.

Twenty minutes later a guy came to fetch me and we wandered upstairs. My back was on the verge of being screwed. All I had to do for relief was get to Superdrug round the corner.

I can't make any swift or sudden movements when it goes, must stay calm. If not I'll put it into spasm and be completely locked for forty minutes.

When we got to the second floor the guy ran around the corridors, peeking inside rooms to see if one was free. After five or six peeks we stumbled across an empty one and went in.

He was a good guy. We talked about my drinking, smoking dope and the impending requirement for my staying clean and sober for 28 days before entering the gambling clinic. He thought it was a tall order when I told him about the holiday. I agreed. He reckoned he might be able to get some psychologists on me and that I could try AA again. Anything to break the habit. He suggested that a respectable reduction in my drinking might be the best option.

At the end he asked about consent. One box was for information to be passed on, essentially, to the state and private firms. I declined. The other was to agree that my information was confidential and would not leave their service.

'That's a bit of a wind up, isn't it? One asks for permission to use my information, the other says it's completely confidential.'

'They pay the bills so we have to ask.'

We went downstairs and said goodbye, then I went off to Superdrug for the relief. There was a queue at the pharmacy and all I wanted was the high strength ibuprofen. I was irate and impatient, mumbling to myself. Unhappy.

After a fried breakfast in the market, gobbling down a pill with coffee, I decided to go back home and take the day off. The scaffold was going up the next day so I'd be out in the open as far as Gerry's concerned.

The story is, I've done a bit of work for Gerry over the past few months. He's another painter and about three months ago he asked me to go and quote for a job in Notting Hill so I did. I really thought I'd get it. The guy at the house was cool and I love working in that area, right close to Portobello.

I gave my price to Gerry, he added his percentage and quoted the customer. After a few days, I asked if he'd put in the quote to the guy and he said yes. But then Gerry and I had a tiff and fell out, so I heard nothing back.

About a month or two later, I was in Notting Hill so I decided to drop in at the house and see about the painting. It hadn't been done so it was worth a try.

He answered the door and invited me in. It turned out he'd never received the quote from Gerry so he'd gone with another painter. I asked what his price was and it was just shy of mine. He gave me his email to send a quote for the work, just in case the other guy went wrong.

As it happened, Gerry called up a few weeks after that and I started doing bits of work for him again, just on a day rate. Having a whole hour to kill at lunchtime meant going to the pub for two or three pints in the garden. It was a bad habit to form but most enjoyable.

Then the guy from Notting Hill called to say the other painter couldn't get scaffolding. Could I and did I want the job?

Did I? Oh yes! And that's how I got this job I'm on.

I've been wondering how and when to tell Gerry but it's all his own doing because he never even bothered sending the quote. At one time, when I still hadn't received the call from the customer, I told Gerry I'd been to see him when I was in the area. He was ok about it but said it wasn't cool. He reaffirmed that he'd sent the quote and that it was declined but I had a funny feeling he was telling fibs and that it would come off in the end.

I've since told Gerry that I've got another job down in Guildford and that I'll be entering rehab in October so I won't be doing any more work for him till January. He was cool about it but I really must tell him straight what happened. Have I pinched a job from under his nose? Answers on a postcard, please.

With the scaffold going up tomorrow at front of house, I'll be visible, and I don't want Gerry finding out that way so I need to tell him I got the job. Should I give him a kickback on this one? I still don't know.

Having started the job last Friday, all the work so far has been at the back of the house, apart from that little bit of scraping on the railings.

The scaffolder called the next day to say he couldn't put it up till Saturday so I carried on elsewhere, bringing things forward with care to my lower back, which had fully recovered.

On Saturday I got to work for the usual 8am start. The scaffolders arrived at 10 and were gone by 1 so I went to The Elgin for a few Hells and a salad, then crossed the road for Paddy Power, playing and losing on Centurion. I won a race at Warwick and did a three-way acca with Chelsea, Spurs and Man City.

Everyone was huffing and puffing and whispering hatred at their machines. No one was winning.

I'm sure there must be certain times when the machines just don't pay. One server told me they pay out liberally one week and not the other, making it impossible to win. This got me thinking how easy it would be for those in the know to be told when to lump large on the machines, winning a pile. It's the same in big business so why not gambling? They're all at it.

I went back to work till 4 then trotted off for pints and food at The Castle. It turned out that the Coral close to the house hadn't closed down, it had just shut for carnival, so I went there, won a hundred on a horse and then lost a few hundred on Hercules.

Back at work till 7 I asked for another advance. Happy with the work so far he made a transfer into my account there and then.

At The Lonsdale, the barman, who knew I liked a full pint from previous occasions, told me that the manager had decreed a 10% minimum head on all lagers but he still served it to the brim. My pint, my rules!

Man City screwed my acca so that was another fifty down the hole. The other two came right and if City hadn't drawn I'd have been two hundred up and back in the game.

At the Notting Hill Gate Coral I lost fifty on some American nag and then started playing Hercules. After about ten minutes it had rinsed three hundred in cash off me so I went up to the till and asked for fifty to be put on the same machine. That went in about two minutes so I asked for another forty, again on the card. When that went straight through I did what I never do and kicked a large metal stool to the floor, walking out in a rage.

When I looked at my account with a pint at The Old Swan it was down to forty-two quid, which meant I was down the six hundred the customer had just transferred. Taking out forty at the cashpoint on the corner I played the fruity with another pint, both of which went in minutes.

It always seems otherworldly when I find myself skint after working so hard but I've only got myself to blame. The lady's back from holiday in a few days so I can always ask her for a bit to tide me by.

The next morning, Sunday, I woke up creaky. I've started to use my hand as support to get out of bed. My lower back isn't what it was and requires extra help. With no money for food, roll ups or the tube, I took the car in to work and called my sister. I asked how much was left in my children's account and she told me there was one hundred and forty so I asked for sixty to be transferred that day and sixty the next day, saying I wouldn't feel the need to gamble if it came in drips and drabs. I had to pay for the ULEZ. She wasn't convinced but made the transfer anyway.

Since the scaffolding's been up I've been fantasising that I'll fall off and get myself impaled on the front railings. If I went from the top level I'd be killed instantly. It's a big enough drop to slice me in half with no chance of survival, but if I went off from the first or second level I might have second thoughts on the way down and negotiate the fall to avoid the railings, a fate worse than death.

The top level of scaffolding is a very dodgy affair. There's a strip of masonry right at the top of the building that needs attention but the scaffolding doesn't reach it by a long way so

I've had to hire a set of ladders to get up there. The boards are well placed so it's easy enough to get there but hairy on the way up and there's nowhere for tools or the roller tray so I have to perch them on an adjoining set of steps. This is my last day of drinking and smoking dope and gambling. Thankfully I'm almost broke so there's no money to burn.

With Man Utd playing Arsenal I finished up and watched the first half at The Elgin, almost getting into a fight with a surly United fan who took pleasure in the terrible fouling of Martinelli by McTominay, which was surely a red card but went unpunished by the referee, also from Manchester.

At half-time I drove down to The Hansom Cab to watch the second half in peace but it had been taken over. Once the only spit and sawdust pub left in Kensington proper, it was now a placid Thai food joint. It seems that the rich areas don't need to entice people into their pubs any more. Gentrification has torn through towns and cities, leaving the indigenous working class Brit with smelly Wetherspoons and even smellier social clubs, if they managed to survive the property gangsters.

The Asian lady at The Cab said there were plenty of places to watch the match in Earl's Court but that would be a rowdy affair so I went to a pub I know on North End Road. It turned out this place had been taken over too, but in a good way. A proper Chelsea football haunt, the new landlady had gone back to its roots.

She had the crooner karaoke on for the old people in the main room. In the back room there were three screens and one in the garden, all for the football, so I was a pig in shit. Moretti was £4.80 and there was only one other guy watching the match, which was still locked at 1-1.

When I went out for a roll up and United scored I heard the other guy celebrating with a mean gravelly cheer. I winced. They'd bullied and cheated all through the match and we'd had a superb individual Martinelli strike disallowed because of an innocuous challenge in the lead up to the goal. When they went three-one up I knew it was game over so I went and watched the karaoke shenanigans with another pint in the front room. Those old school English landladies know how to put smiles on faces, and the pints are always full.

I went for a final one at The Sporting Page but they were still cashless so that was me screwed. As I walked out, someone at the bar said he'd stand me a pint so I had one with him. He was from Merseyside and hated United so we had a good old moan about the game.

I parked the car up at home and went to see if the boys were outside the bookies for one last joint but it was a completely different set of people there. One offered me a tenner bag so I told him I was giving it up the next day and only wanted a joint's worth, to which he told me in no uncertain terms to fuck off. I'd have done the same in his shoes.

After that I went to Sainsburys to laugh at the prices and walk straight through without buying anything (a new habit), then to the Caribbean place for a fish and rice dish with the last of my money. These days, all the new wave burger places and takeaways want at least a tenner and then the fries are four quid on top, whereas The Kebab Kid on New Kings Road still does its excellent lamb sharwarma for just shy of six quid with fresh vegetables and all the spices.

The next day was Monday 5th of September, my first clean and sober day of the twenty-eight leading up to rehab. With the lady back in town, I worked the morning, had the ladders sent back and then took the tube home at midday. On the way up the hill I stopped off at Tesco by the prison for smoked salmon but they've stopped selling it because it keeps getting pinched so I had to settle on ham for the sandwiches. The soup we like wasn't there so I got some other brand. Back at the flat the lady arrived as I was having a bath so she gave me a back scrub and we chatted about things. She was very keen to know how I'd cope over the next month.

When I got out of the bath and put a t-shirt on I started to sweat profusely so I had to take it off. It ripped as it pulled against my sticky torso and the lady laughed, telling me my beer belly would be gone at the month's end. I tried putting on shorts but the sweat wouldn't have it so I had to lie down on the bed. The lady came and sat next to me and I told her I'd be fine, that she mustn't give it a thought. I could see her concern. After a cuddle I made sure she understood that it would be counter-productive for her to bring up the subject of whether I'd had a drink or a smoke. Any infraction would be reported.

She'd put me in touch with the medium and wanted to see my cards, which I'd taken a photo of. We went through the reveal and then talked about the clinic and Lambeth drug and alcohol service. I didn't tell her about the guy suggesting I reduce rather than quit the alcohol completely because I didn't want her worrying about me using that as an excuse to go overboard. Her holiday turned out fine but she'd had to keep up with her kids on the drink front as they're hot on the cocktails now. Before she left I poured the last of a bottle of Amaretto into the sink.

It's got so cloak and dagger I can't even walk her down the hill nowadays. I can't let her be found out by prying eyes and the whole charade has put a strain on our time together outside of the flat. We used to trot around everywhere but that's all changed now.

On Tuesday morning I made coffee for the first time in ages and took it with me instead of going to Greggs. I even had a piece of toast before I left. I slept very well but that would have only been because the day before last was a big drinking day. I know it won't always be that easy to sleep without a drink or a smoke because the old head can keep ticking over.

What I'd really like is to be able to walk past a bookies or a fruit machine without feeling that crazy urge to gamble. I'd like to feel no fear, anger or resentment for the pain gambling has caused me, to wipe the slate clean and start afresh. I'd like to be completely blind to all aspects of gambling, to forget the hundreds of thousands lost.

A gamble-free life is my ultimate freedom. In pubs I've never been able to properly engage in conversation when a fruit machine's winking at me. In the end, it always gets its way.

I admit to having a strange brain. From about sixteen and for a fair few years I'd go and watch Arsenal from my spot in the North Bank. The mass of all those football fans was overwhelming and I'd look around the stadium in awe. Then my imagination would take over and I'd wonder how deep in shit the stadium would be if everyone's craps throughout their lifetimes were piled into the place. This thought would arrive unprovoked and only once during a match. I'd guess at where the shit would stop; up to certain levels on the two adjacent stands, or butting up against the hoardings of the upper stand, or halfway up the huge clock at the Clock End, overflowing the North Bank and into the streets.

On Wednesday I worked the morning and then met the lady at the flat. Knowing I was off to Crete the next day, we had a good time together, chatting gently with a light lunch, saying farewell in our way.

I'd found a mini laptop through a guy that runs a computer repairs shop in Guildford so I hopped in the car and drove down to collect it. He'd put Word on the thing and it seemed right enough so I bought it for sixty quid, then drove back home for an early night.

The flight was fine and I sat with a friendly old couple. They asked what I did and I told them I was a painter and a writer on the side. They asked if I'd published anything and for the first time in ages I opened up about the Queen book.

Instead of taking a taxi, I walked to the bus depot and waited for the next one to take me to the beach resort. A friend of the lady had booked it all for me and in a brief account of the hotel it said it was 150 yards to the beach.

After climbing up a hill for 500 yards I was sweating and panting (because of smoking, my ability to walk up hills has taken a nosedive in recent years).

When I saw the room I was livid. The place resembled very basic student accommodation, a far cry from the pictures on the net. The door was the only source of air. I complained when I felt the bed, one big set of springs. The owner seemed intent on ignoring anything I said, placing cards for his mates' restaurants and scooter hire companies on a little table. I told him I needed to take a shower and reiterated that I was in no way happy with the room.

There was no wall attachment for the showerhead so I dowsed myself down quickly, dried, got dressed and stormed out to look for another hotel.

There was another place a short walk away and the lady there called around but everywhere was full, then I met a young guy who ran another place further down the hill and he started calling around for me. After a few minutes he found someone called Maria who had a room and would pick me up in thirty minutes from the minimart on the main road. I said yes and walked back to the hotel, calling the owner on the way. In the end he gave me an apartment on the first floor so I raced back to tell the guy to call it off with Maria. There were no hard feelings.

Settling in, I got to work on the mini laptop but after writing twenty words it froze. I tried again and managed sixty but then it froze again. Calling the guy in Guildford he suggested a few things but nothing worked. The laptop was a dud.

I went out for a walk, to look around the place, wandering down to the main beach area. It was awash with cars and tourists and coaches, little slivers of pebbly beach full to the brim with bodies. I wouldn't go there again. On the way back I decided to look for a notepad but every supermarket told me the same thing; they used to sell them but there was no demand any more. Eventually, I found a children's scribbling pad and went back to the hotel for a nap.

Arsenal were playing in Europe that evening so I headed down the hill to look for a screen. The only one I could find was in a hotel and when I approached the bar a woman came up to me and said the facilities were for guests only. I said I'd buy a soft drink and she caved in when I told her my team was the one playing on the telly.

The moment I sat down a text arrived from the lady to say the Queen had passed away. I had to read it a few times for it to sink in.

The next day I found a great little beach with its own restaurant. As I was on my own the sets of sun loungers were half-price so I treated myself to one right by the shoreline and had an excellent linguine with clams and mussels for lunch. Also fortuitous was that I'd taken a coffee at breakfast time at a café on the way to the beach. It had a mini library in the pool room, from where I plucked out *10lb Penalty* by Dick Francis.

By the end of the day I was a happy puppy, knowing that my time could be filled with reading and sunbathing far away from crowds. Writing the journal was no longer an option.

Back at the hotel I tried writing a poem in the scribbling pad. I had a title for it, *Falling Awake*, but I hadn't made a record of thoughts at the time they'd come, so my attempt was half-arsed and cack-handed. In summary, it was meant to be about how easy it is to fear and not love, emotionally asleep in our waking hours, removed from ourselves, but I couldn't even do that.

The next day, Saturday, was a copy of the previous day. All the football matches had been cancelled as a mark of respect for the Queen's passing so there was no temptation to find a bar. I finished *10lb Penalty*, a brilliant little crime mystery, and went to exchange it for another at the café on the way back to the hotel. The next one was an equally good read by Charles Willeford, *The Shark-Infested Custard*, about four men who lived in the same building in Miami, revealing the dark side of The American Dream just as it was starting to crack.

Sunday and Monday were taken at the beach, reading on a lounger with linguine for lunch. I suppose I'm a creature of habit. Structure's good for changing brain patterns, offering a different set of rewards to keep buoyant. I hadn't really thought about booze at all. At around five I went back to the hotel for a shower and a nap and then headed out again for supper.

The place I tried on the first night was underwhelming but on the second night I found a good, traditional place, which I continued to frequent for my sea bream. I hadn't drunk a thing for a whole week and felt good. The beer belly was going and my head was becoming clearer with every passing thought.

On the eighth day of being clean and sober, Tuesday, I had an altercation at a hotel and something snapped in my head. Every time I saw a glass of white wine or an ice-cold beer being delivered to someone on a lounger, my heart fell and howled with contempt. When I sat down in the restaurant for lunch, my eyes were drawn to glasses on other tables. In the afternoon, I read the end of *The Shark-Infested Custard* but by then I was in my own newly processed soup. It was bubbling away anxiously, setting dirtily around the edges.

On the way back to the hotel I stopped in at the café to exchange the Willeford for another, this time *Running with The Firm* by James Bannon.

Up till that day I'd always get a large bottle of water and some nuts at the minimart on the corner that led up to the hotel, but this time, when I got to the fridges, I stopped at the one full of beer bottles and took a look inside without opening the door. I thought of my promise to stay sober, to go to rehab in pursuit of a better life, to get a proper grip on the gambling, but then I thought of that word, 'reduction'. I had been encouraged to reduce my intake and this represented a fair reward to celebrate a week of abstinence.

Pressing the fuck-it button the door to the beers opened and I took out two large bottles, one Mythos and one Alpha.

The moment they were in my hands was utter relief. Taking a bottle of water from the adjoining fridge I paid up and left.

Back at the hotel I placed one of the beers in the freezer and cracked open the other, pouring the sparkling contents into a pint glass. Placing it on a table in the bedroom I opened up the scribbling pad and started to write. Here it is;

I thought I'd celebrate the continuance of my sobriety with a couple of beers. This is my eighth day of twenty-eight till I go to the gambling clinic and I'm on the island of Crete. I've been here five days and this morning, in a text, I promised the lady I'd seek out a nice English breakfast somewhere so out I went at around 10.30.

The first place I stopped at, just before the main road, had a pool and you can be there all day swanning around for five euros so when I saw they did an English breakfast I went in. The woman at the bar started getting all the ingredients out of fridges and freezers. Seeing the frozen sausages and the mega-tin of mushroom slices sloshing around in brine I told her not to worry and scarpered, just as she was about to open the microwave to zap the sausages. Coffee was included in the price but it was instant.

Next stop was the hotel I'd watched the Arsenal swat Zurich on my first night. I knew it had a 'guests only' policy but when I saw a massive advertising board outside on the main road, announcing English breakfast and all manner of other glories, I thought they might have slackened the policy now that the high season had passed. Maybe it was just different in the day as opposed to the evening. Why else would they advertise right there on the street?

Sliding open the gate and passing by the pool, I said good morning to the woman who'd let me watch the match. She looked at me, did that awful tut, a sort of sucking tut, and wagged a finger at me.

'You can't be here,' she said, with a crooked little smile. 'It's guests only'.

'So why's there a sign outside advertising English breakfast?'

'That's for *guests*.'

By this time, her beefy boyfriend, who'd been standing at the far end of the bar with a slovenly look of disdain, made his way over to put in his tuppence worth.

I got in first as he waded over. 'Why have you got a fuckin' board advertising English breakfast outside, on the main road, when it's for guests only?'

He took immediate offence to the F-word (it seemed to have almost crippled him) but I wasn't stopping there.

'It's like advertising a bar you can't go into. It's fuckin' ridiculous!'

In a bid to stop smoking, or at the very least see how the day fared without a fag now that I was 'in a good place', I'd left the roll ups at the hotel. Bad move.

'You need to leave,' he said, raising his voice. A few punters who were eating breakfast in a little alcove turned and looked over at us.

'You're an idiot.'

'Leave now!'

'Oh, I'm leaving alright, but you need to take that fuckin' stupid, misleading board away unless you want me to throw it in the *guests only* pool.'

'I'll call the police if you don't get out of here.'

'Go fuck yourself.'

'You go fuck yourself!'

'Piss off.'

And that's how I left. As I walked away I felt an awful desire to throw a bar stool or two at the bottles of drink carefully arranged behind the bar. That would keep him busy for a while.

He said fuck you once more, probably hoping for a decent

rebuttal, but I was gone. He shouted again that he'd call the police and tell them about my behaviour. I said nothing, leaving the sliding gate open as I made my way to the main road.

At the minimart I got a ham and cheese toastie thing, wolfed it down ravenously, bought some roll ups, papers, filters and a lighter, then ordered a takeaway cappuccino. I was shaking from a potent mixture of fear and anger, the smoke and caffeine doing little to alleviate my dread.

Stood there on the main drag, I was in quandary, puffing away to arrest thoughts of the police driving past, spotting me and screeching to a halt to question me about the scene I'd caused at the hotel with the wankers.

I was stupidly caught between going back to the apartment (for some reason, I thought I should hide my debit card, driving licence, wallet photos of the kids, passport, flat keys and cash) and just going to the beach?

If the guy I'd told to fuck off really wanted to gain revenge he could easily find out where I was staying, just by asking around about the loner English bloke. Being the only solo traveller in the resort, I'd be easy to track down. If he chose to, he could break into the apartment, steal my belongings and make the rest of my holiday an absolute misery.

After one more roll up at the minimart, I decided to go to the beach. It wasn't an easy time and I spent the first hour waiting for the cops to come and pull me off the lounger in front of everyone.

After lunch I went back up the hill to hide my stuff, finding a great little place behind a make-do shelf in the kitchen, sliding all my paraphernalia up there. I think they'll come out easily with the aid of a knife jammed and bent outwardly. The cash is under the sink in a little groove between the aluminium and worktop.

I'm always overcautious in hotels because a friend nicked a load of money from me after a rave in Paris back in the nineties.

I'd fallen asleep and left the door open, or maybe he'd had it opened by staff, I don't know. Anyway, he'd taken the money and in the morning I found my shoes tied to the exhaust pipe of the old Austin 1100.

Another reason I'm weird about leaving stuff in hotel rooms is because I did the same thing as my mate, funnily enough here in Crete back in the eighties. A couple of Finnish girls, one of whom I'd shagged, told me to meet them in their hotel room but they weren't there. It was my last night at the resort and I was almost out of cash. They'd given me a key so I waited a while but no girls returned so I looked in a bedside drawer and found about three hundred quid in cash. It was too much to pass up so I took it and escaped via the balcony, thinking it safer than leaving by the door and taking the stairs. Bad move. There was someone on the next balcony and he called out to me just as I shimmied and jumped.

Rather than running down the driveway, knowing he'd see me in my tartan-checkered trousers (a Simple Minds-influenced purchase), I elected to go up into the woods. I stayed there all night, praying the cops wouldn't come and get me. There were rats, mice and mosquitoes all over the place so I didn't sleep a wink. At about 5am I scurried down the driveway and made it to the student place where I'd left my stuff. I waited around till six to get my bag, then caught the bus back to the airport, where I bought a ticket to I can't remember.

After hiding the stuff, I went back to the beach to get more rays on the lounger. As you've probably guessed I'm as paranoid as a rat in a sewer. It's been this way since very early childhood but it really took off with the introduction of drugs, aged sixteen. That's when it got to be fun, but while I'm very fond of and grateful for my imagination, it's certainly taken its toll over the years. Every day is a battle of wits against whichever demon shows up. There's a fair few angels in attendance so I can't complain.

I still haven't felt much for the Queen's death, which is odd because I've always liked her. Princess Diana's death was a different matter. I was in Paris when her car crashed in the tunnel. The day after, I was so out of it that I asked a friend to drive the Austin and he ended up smashing it into the back of a taxi by the Seine. The taxi driver came out and took the keys out of the dashboard. Then he called the cops so I told my mate to scarper (he ran all the way back to his squat). I was taken in and put in a cell, where I slept comatose. When an officer came down to let me go much later on, I threw up all over the stairs.

There were couples chinking glasses and laughing together and every time I went for a dip in the sea all I could see on the shoreline were glasses shimmering in the sunlight, perched on little tables between loungers. I suppose I made my mind up at about 4pm, after which I shuffled about looking at crap on Facebook.

At precisely 5.22pm I'd had enough and heaved myself up from the lounger. I knew what I'd do and I did it.

In hindsight, it's easy to forget signs that lead us down the wrong track. The hotel altercation set me back onto the road of self-destruct. That powerful mix of fear, anger, resentment and shame had won the day for the nth time.

One beer down and the other in the pint glass, I could easily take it or leave it, but it's there so I know what I'll do. I'm looking at the bubbles in the glass and sighing, half ruing my decision to drink.

It's the next day now. I feel fuzzy and old. I woke up at half six and took relief for a tetchy headache. Looking into the bathroom mirror I couldn't believe what I saw, my face wrinkled and blotchy from yesterday's intake, which I eventually ran up to five pints. Around my eyes, the dried out skin made for deep lines and the bags under my eyes were the worst I'd ever seen. My neck was wrinkled and looked thinner when I gulped.

I went back to bed and woke up again at nine, had coffee and cereal. Again I looked at my face in the bathroom mirror, the ravages of alcohol still there. It scared the crap out of me.

It's been a good holiday and I was drink-free till yesterday afternoon but my little stumble has had the desired effect. Now I'm back on the wagon. By having a bellyful I can discern of two positively important factors about my alcoholism, which I know I'll have to live with till the day I die.

The first is that, with or without a drink, I was just as self-conscious at the fish restaurant down the road. For four nights I'd eaten stone cold sober. During these evenings I'd sit at my table with all the couples and groups around me, happy to people-watch, waiting for lovely food. If there was kindly eye contact I returned it. An inquisitive kid might stare at me, probably wondering why I was alone when everyone else was in company, and the odd cat would sit at my feet waiting for scraps. It's easy to tell myself that I'm more comfortable in these situations with a drink on board, but I can now categorically say that's not the case.

By the time I arrived at the restaurant last night I'd had three pints (one at the mini library bar on the way) so I was well on course. Sitting down at a table, I realised I was just as self-conscious as the times before, if not more. The only difference was how I managed that shyness. With booze on board I people-watched as normal but then shyness took hold with quite a fierce grip and I could barely look up. Admittedly, my fourth beer was going down very well with the olives and garlic bread.

Across the way, I saw there was another solo diner, a young woman. She was attractive, not my type but she looked like fun. As much as I wanted to invite her to sit with me I couldn't even look at her once the initial friendly eye contact had been made so when she got up to leave, passing by my table, I froze. If I'd been sober I'd certainly not have been as bashful but, conversely, the opportunity probably wouldn't have arisen unless I was under the spell of beer. Such are the mysteries of life.

I could far better analyse other parties at tables when sober, and was far less prone to lazy judging. There was always one couple whose manner suggested complete and reciprocal boredom, but never more than one. The other parties were generally happy in each other's company. All were affable to waiting staff.

Methodical and well practised in the extraction of meat from the sea bream, I found that I was now expert in its devouring, with only two very minor bones making it to my mouth during the entire operation. Beer or no beer, I could navigate a fish just as well either way.

The second important factor in my drinking experiment is that, gawping at my hideous reflection this morning, it's crystal clear that my body will no longer abide imbibement gracefully. Somehow, I need to find a way to stay sober.

The only unhappy revelation in this drinking experiment is that I only felt that lovely urge to write when I had the beer next to me. The scariest thing about sobriety is that I'll lose my sense of humour and settle into a mediocre life without much colour or impulsion.

I'll be going home tomorrow. With no bookies about, I haven't thought about gambling for a whole week. I'm keen to get on with the house in Notting Hill teetotal but, already, I'm looking to Saturday as my next drinking and gambling day, what with the football back on and me being in my favourite spot. 'Reduction' suddenly feels like a blessing.

I don't generally keep friends, apart from Kieran, and when I go out to the pubs I like the freedom to come and go as I please (which is probably as a result of my fruit machine addiction). With the flavour on I'm most happy traipsing around on a solo pub machine crawl, happening upon strangers I like (or dislike) for transient banter.

Maybe, now that I've taken a drink, I can reveal to my guy at the clinic that the bloke at Lambeth drug and alcohol service suggested reduction rather than complete abstinence. I'm not sure he'll buy it but let's see. After all, it was the clinic that wanted me to seek external advice and that's what he said. Whatever happens, I'm not going to lie to him when we speak in a week's time.

*

It felt good to be home. Just one bit of mail now the world's gone paperless and that was from the boiler people wanting to service the heating in the flat.

I went to work the next day and started on the ground floor and basement area at the front. I wanted to get the above sections done before I left for Crete so that the scaffolding could be removed but it hadn't been possible. I texted the scaffolder before the holiday and asked if he could remove it this coming weekend so I can get on in the basement without having to work around all the poles. He didn't bother replying, so I got onto him again but he didn't answer, then I left another text reiterating the need for it to be gone at the weekend, which again he didn't reply to. I only did a half-day as I was seeing the lady at the flat in the afternoon.

Friday was a full day spent prepping up the walls of the basement, which were in a worse state than I thought. One of them had suffered from water ingress after a recent flood so I removed the paintwork.

The scaffolder had placed a pole right in front of the door to the basement flat, which denied access completely. The customer rented the flat on a short-term basis through a local agent so he wasn't too happy. As luck would have it, he hadn't received any bookings but it was shoddy work, totally unacceptable. I couldn't get to the door and its metal security gate to prep it up and that started to piss me off. I kept banging my head on poles and felt like a pinball in a machine.

The customer asked about the scaffolding and I told him I'd get back onto him for a firm date.

On the Saturday, he went off to the country at about ten so I had the house to myself. I couldn't face working in the basement so I got started on the front door and its surround.

At eleven I went for a falafel in Portobello. The stall next to the falafel man had a fat-fryer that was spewing dirty oil smoke all over the market so I had a word with the guy but he ignored me. The girl at the falafel stand said she had to breathe his fat smoke in all day so I had another, much more insistent word and he got the message, turning the fryer off. I left in an angry state of mind, batting away thoughts of an early beer. It's only the twelfth day of my supposed sobriety, but it has to be said that in terms of a reduction I've completely reversed my drinking pattern. Instead of six days on and one day off, I was now drinking one day a week or thereabouts.

I scoffed the falafel at the house and felt a bit better but my mind was still firmly fixed on the impending prospect of a beer and a bet. In the time it took to make good the front door after removing furniture, filling tiny cracks and dinks with epoxy resin and sanding down with finishing paper, my mouth must have produced a pint's worth of saliva in anticipation of a beer. By midday, the door was ready for an undercoat so I put that on with aplomb.

I went to The Wellington at one and the barmaid was rude so I drained the pint and hoofed it down to The Castle, where I had two more in quick succession. I sat outside smoking. A Jamaican guy was at the next table so I told him about my new plan, to go and live on a Jamaican beach or in a pop-up tent in a rich person's garden, doing bits of painting to pay my way. I'd go directly after completing rehab in January because I detest winter. The thought of coming out, going back to Brixton and returning to work is too horrible to contemplate. If I'm to stay sober I'll need a real break and Jamaica seems the perfect place for a good six-week sortie, returning with spring around the corner. The Jamaican guy approved of my little plan.

After the pub I steamed into the bookies and won a ton on Hercules, made a ten pound accumulator on the footy and went back to work on a brick wall in the back garden.

Over the years this wall had become infected by damp and the mortar joints were in a sorry state. To hack out those joints with the tungsten scraper is extremely satisfying. With the dead mortar out I swept and bagged it up and then hosed the whole wall down, getting into the joints to clear out the loose debris. A highly satisfying task, knowing it would dry clean as a whistle for filling.

The scaffolder finally called. They're a breed apart and you don't want to rub them up the wrong way, especially when you find a good one.

The footy acca was an instant loser with the early kick-off going wrong. I sanded the iron railings at front of house and painted the fleur de lis before leaving at six, off to The Lonsdale, thinking I'd call it a day after one.

I sat outside and got talking to an American woman. She was a Buddhist who'd spent eighteen years in India, skipping from one ashram to another in a quest for spiritual enlightenment, most definitely a trustafarian.

I told her about my concept for the afterlife; how one's conduct during life defines it. Like with hotels, I had a star system that went something like this; if you'd led a good, honest life and battled hard with a great many adversities, remaining true to yourself and never complying to the wickedness of the world's ways, then you got a five-star afterlife. Because in life you thrived from encouragement and made the most of your attributes, bringing joy to others, you would be allowed to accompany your still alive loved ones. Wherever they went, you could follow. Although you couldn't communicate together, you could protect loved ones in ways unknown to that living being, guiding them silently through the hardest of times and enjoying their better moments. You could also flit to wherever the hell you wanted to go in the entire universe, and for as long as you liked, engaging with other angels from the same five-star category.

The four-star afterlife is nowhere near as good. In life, while your moral grounding was firm, you were quite rigid in your views and did little to help those less fortunate. For this, while you can be with your living loved ones, you can't adjust their navigation so readily or to such good effect. You certainly can't flit about the universe like you own it but, essentially, the world is still your oyster.

Three-star angels get to meddle with those still alive who had done them wrong, but only to a certain degree. They are, in essence, little flies to annoy their living enemies and, once they too die, the three-star angel is demoted to its two-star companion, with whom they can neither talk or fly. Although the three-star angel can view their living loved ones, nothing at all can be done to help them, almost a fate worse than their own. The afterlife they receive is rewarded for their own lackadaisical conduct throughout life.

The two-star afterlife is no good at all. They sit amongst their own in a world of boring, dull chaos. Once in a while, they can follow three-star angels but, due to the humdrum nature of their afterlife, that opportunity is usually missed. To most two-stars, it's almost not even worth having an afterlife but some thrive in the boring chaos, seeing goodness when it arrives in its very limited way, bringing some cheer to their counterparts. Particularly vibrant two-stars can be promoted to the status of a three-star angel but they quickly abuse this entitlement, at which time they're demoted to being a one-star.

A one-star sits alone in a confined cubicle from which he or she can never leave. There is no escape from this afterlife but they at least get to think their own thoughts.

The American woman asked if I thought every living being got an afterlife and I laughed.

'Are you kidding? Loads of people don't get one!'

She offered to buy me a pint so I said yes. An odd part of my paranoia is that whenever a stranger wants to buy me a drink, I imagine they'll poison me with some guff. This feeling has been with me for thirty years but I still accept drinks to defy the paranoia. I've been drugged with GHB twice and it's not very nice.

We talked for a while but her mood changed (which got me thinking paranoid again). I had the impression I'd somehow offended her, what with the drinks taking effect and the anger of my day still rested within me.

When I got to Notting Hill Gate, I stopped just outside the entrance to the tube and stood there for a minute. How many times have I done that?

If I went down and in I could easily go home and watch the box. Match of The Day would be on later and I could get something decent from the Caribbean place or maybe splash out on an Indian.

But then I saw The Old Swan winking at me from across the road. In my mind's eye the deep blue signage of William Hill flooded my inner vision. Obviously I went to the bookies first, where I won a ton on a dog with my first bet. Well oiled with the pints and about two hundred up on the day, I felt flash but then I lost a load on a couple of American races so I steamed up to the cashpoint on the corner to get some more readies.

Back at the bookies I went back on Centurion and it drained the lot in no time so I put two hundred on the machine with a card, which was rinsed in half an hour. I went back to the cashpoint and found there was only a hundred quid left in the account.

I took out eighty, leaving twenty in for the bastard TV licence, then waddled off to The Old Swan to lick my wounds with a pint of Hells. I tanked that down and went back to Hills.

There was an American horse called Faction Writer at Churchill Downs so I put forty on that and it won by a good ten lengths.

Faction Writer clawed back one-twenty so I lumped fifty on the next race at Belmont Park on a horse called She's My Beauty but it came stone last. Bloody favourites.

Back at The Swan I nursed another pint on a fruit machine and won sixty. The thing with old school fruit machines is that if you get a half decent win it won't pay diddly squat afterwards so I drained the pint and went back to Hills, where I lost my load on Centurion in under ten minutes. Reaching into my jacket pocket I found enough for a pint and went back to the pub.

Sitting outside, I saw that I'd received a few texts from the lady, wondering why I'd gone quiet since the afternoon. She gets worried when I don't answer texts, thinking I've got into a fight with a dickhead in a pub, which I always seem to swerve.

It's odd. I don't even hear the text ping when I'm on a roll. Maybe it's just too noisy in the pub or the bookies. I don't know.

I sent a text back saying I was 'about to go home shortly after a busy day'. I don't like to give away too many details about my shenanigans till I see her or speak to her. That way she doesn't worry too much. She's been very understanding about my two splurges (I told her I'd have some beers that morning). Two in twelve days is pretty damn good really.

I took the tube to Brixton and felt a massive hole in my tummy, having forgotten to eat after the falafel. Seeing the KFC by my bus stop I realised I hadn't had a zinger burger for about three years so I went in and got one as a meal deal, using up the last fiver available in my account.

The zinger was a pathetically small chicken breast (probably sliced in half) with a dollop of mayonnaise and some tired lettuce between two damp patties. The chips, all seventeen of them, were floppy and tasteless. Never again.

I was hungover the next morning but got up and had a quick cup of tea before leaving for work in the car at seven-thirty.

It's the Queen's funeral on Monday so I'm getting jittery about traffic. My tummy was growling for food and I'd found a good twenty quid in change on the coffee table, which meant I could stop off at Cafe Parisienne in Battersea on my way to work. Being a Sunday I could park up without having to pay.

The café serves an excellent fry up and cappuccino, going a long way to restore my faith in little independent places that have somehow managed to survive. Most survivors had gone the other way, hiking up prices and taking the quality down, just like the big boys, but not Kazim. I paid up and we chatted outside, putting the world to rights and laughing at how almost all our freedoms had been taken away by those who are unquestionably the real terrorists.

'When an empire's about to burn, they have to resort to all sorts of mad rules to keep us fighting against each other. But they'll be gone soon,' he reckoned.

'I say stick them on an island.'

A true gentleman, he put a couple of plums in a paper bag for me to take away.

I had a nice chat with the customer's wife when I got to the house. Being a headmistress at a big school, I'd passed a copy of my Queen book to her the day before and she'd enjoyed it. We had a plum together.

The journey home was a nightmare. I'd been transferred a couple of hundred earlier in the day so I was sorely tempted to stop off for a beer, which is my normal response to crap traffic. At Ken High Street I decided to circumvent town by heading west towards Olympia and cutting down at North End Road. The lady texted to tell me they'd closed all but one lane of Cromwell Road heading out of town so I sat on the north side of North End Road, waiting to pass the lights, edging past pubs, salivating for a pint.

After a while I crossed the damned Cromwell and stopped off at Waitrose to get odds and sods because the lady's coming over for the Queen's funeral the next morning. She'd got the chicken so all I needed was vegetables and a few treats on the side.

Unfortunately, the place was out of everything. Further down North End Road I saw that my favourite place for pistachios, walnuts, almonds and cashews was still open so I stopped off, scooping up my selection into a plastic bag. Wandsworth Bridge Road was blocked so I went further down New Kings Road and had a Kebab Kid to refuel. Thoughts of having a pint completely dissipated after that beauty and the traffic miraculously cleared. Even Putney Bridge was a breeze!

When I got home at eight I couldn't believe I'd made that arduous two-hour journey without taking a drink. (Just the thought of it is making me want one now.) If I'd had one I'd have had four or five without doubt, laying to rest any chance of sticking to my reduction-reversal program.

Next morning I scurried off to Sainsburys and actually bought things there! As the lady was coming I even got a celebratory pint of milk (£1.05) and a pack of butter (£2.75). Back home I had a bath and shaved, then chopped up the potatoes, carrots and parsnips to put in water, slicing up an onion and some garlic cloves and putting mushrooms in to sweat the lot on a low heat for the gravy.

Once the lady arrived I put the hard veg in the lower section of the oven and she lathered butter all over the chicken, sprinkling salt flakes on it and sticking half a lemon up its arse. I banged it into the oven. By that time, the Queen's funeral procession was underway so we sat on the sofa and watched.

I told her about the guy at Lambeth drug and alcohol suggesting reduction rather than abstinence, and that I'd talk to the pre-treatment therapist on Thursday and open up to him about my two drinking bouts. He'd probably need to call

Lambeth to confirm reduction was suggested, which was fine by me.

If he asked how I was doing with the dope, I could still say I hadn't smoked a thing.

We ate up at about one and went to bed for a good old cuddle.

That week I steamed into the job. On the Tuesday, while I was sat on the pavement painting the footing of the railings, a man came and said hi. He was from Barbados so I told him about my idea of living on a beach. Having thought a little more carefully about it, I realised that, if I had a flight with a return in six weeks and without a hotel booked, I'd need a contact out there in case the authorities pulled me over, so I asked him about my chances of getting clearance without a contact.

He said I needn't worry about that and offered to give me his details over there. He was going for a couple of months in January and would vouch for me if I was pulled over. I scurried off and borrowed a pen from the lady of the house, giving that and the back of a piece of sandpaper to Rocky, the Barbadian man.

He wrote down his name, address and phone number over there and assured me there wouldn't be a problem if they called. That really put a shine on the week.

I only had a drink on Wednesday night, meeting up with the lady and one of her best friends. This was the first time in three and a half years that I'd met any of her friends and pretty much the only reason for that was because she had started an affair too. Empathy comes with shared experience.

When I took the Thursday call from the therapist, I told him about the two drinking bouts. I also told him about the Lambeth man's advice.

He said he was on my side but would have to talk to his people. As I thought, he'd also need to confirm with Lambeth that reduction was suggested as my best option.

On Saturday I went to work as usual and had three pints at

lunchtime. The scaffolder came and took everything down.

After lunchtime I went back for the afternoon till six. Rocky passed by and gave me his London number. He'd already booked his flight for the 24th of January and suggested I do the same before they hiked the prices up. To his mind, the best way would be to book a ticket on the same flight as he and his girlfriend so I'm now seriously considering buying my ticket in advance.

I had a couple more pints after work along with a little gamble. By this time I purposely had very little money and only asked for a small advance to keep me going, having already spent two-thirds of my earnings, which meant there'd be no petrol banger or payback into the girls' account. I'm a shitshow.

When I got back to Brixton I saw that an Itsu had opened up opposite the bus stop so I went and had a look. They pride themselves on openly displaying their food trays for people to choose from and take to the till for payment but at this new one in Brixton everything's behind the counter.

As it was 8.30pm it was half-price time. The server had piled high a load of food trays on the counter for people to choose from so I picked out two sushi trays and sat to eat.

There was a woman at the table next to me and we got talking. She'd been a nurse for thirty-six years and was about to retire. She'd brought up a daughter, who was now just shy of thirty. They'd always lived together but the lady was now thinking of selling her two-bed flat and downsizing to give her daughter a start on the property ladder. I thought this a great idea and suggested a one-bed flat, perhaps with a garden or patio and a bit further out from Brixton. Then she said, so proudly, that she'd mistakenly taken her daughter's debit card to a cashpoint and found that she'd independently amassed a large amount of money. I said she must have done a good job on her and tears came to her eyes.

On Sunday I worked for ten hours straight with a hangover,

clearing the basement area, painting the bay window and the surrounding walls, prepping the door to the flat and coating the metal staircase. Driving home I suddenly realised that rehab was only one week away.

On Monday, still unsure when I'd finish the damn job, the lady came up for lunch and, in a quiet corner of a restaurant close by, we shared a burrata starter followed by fresh pasta with wild truffles, some of which had been burnt.

I went back to work and it started to rain at three so I downed tools for cheap beers at The Pig and Whistle underneath Grenfell Tower. I knew I had to stick to my regime but I felt absolutely wiped out after lunch and the rain was the final straw.

On the way there, an old buddy I'd fallen out with years ago called to say that Chris, his brother and also the illustrator of my Queen book, had died in his flat six weeks ago. I'd seen him at about that time, after he'd called out of the blue. We met at The Falcon and he looked terribly gaunt with big puffy eyes. He'd lost a fair few teeth too.

He was still Chris, though, mild-mannered and painfully soulful. He'd written a book about two lovers escaping an epidemic by living in a forest together. The book ran to four hundred pages, his first attempt at writing, and I asked if he'd like me to read it. Also on his mind was Thames Water, with whom he was in a bitter dispute. Because he only drinks spring water, and after reading about the awful properties of the tap water they regurgitate, he'd refused to pay their extortionate bills for the last year or two. His face fell when I half-jokingly suggested they'd poison it at the mains as revenge for his obstinacy.

Sat with a pint I wondered if he'd died that night I saw him. He hadn't been to a pub for two years, having to drink his vodka at home for lack of cash. I felt terrible when I remembered denying him a double Grey Goose. We'd had a couple of pints of Hells together before parting company for the last time.

News of his death was horrible and it hit me hard. It was also a good reason/excuse to get pissed, which was exactly what I did.

Rain had screwed up my day and I still didn't know exactly when I'd finish the job, which was a bind because I had another job starting on Thursday and I was hoping I'd have Wednesday clear for the lady and a whole day off to recuperate.

The next day, Tuesday, I got in by seven-thirty and put a second coat to the walls in the basement. By lunchtime I'd done that, glossed the bay window and also blacked the trim at the bottom of the now lovely whiter than white walls, masking up with low tack tape to give a perfect line.

All I had to do was take up the tape from the floor and then paint one final coat on the metal staircase and the entire basement would be finished, leaving me with a few touches on windows around the house to sign off the whole job.

Just as I'd got to the top of the stairs, applying the last lick of paint, a massive downpour fell from the sky. I watched helplessly as the black trim slowly disappeared, filling the basement floor with runny deep grey water. The staircase, now awash with blackened rainwater, dripped down and splashed onto all the surrounding walls. Grabbing one of my cotton twill dust sheets I tried to wipe the walls but it just smeared it in. To make matters worse my left knee was throbbing, having failed to properly click back into position while I was taping the floor. It had always clicked back in till now so this was a turn for the worse. It took a good twenty seconds of straightening to get it back in and it ached when it finally found its place. With this new development in my body's deterioration, I was now in deep trouble if I was to rely on painting to keep me afloat. The hangover can't have helped but it was clear that rehab was coming at a crucial time in my little old life.

Anyway, it was all hands on deck. I got the sweep and a bucket from indoors, racing back to the front door. Just as I got there

I slipped and landed on my arse. The bucket broke so I had to knock on a neighbour's door and borrow theirs.

Thankfully, there was a tap in the basement so I filled up the bucket and splashed it around the floor amid showers that further ruined the morning's work. After about half an hour of that, the black trim had all but disappeared. Crucially, though, the rain had stopped and all the seeping black had been swept into the drain, saving the appearance of the floor, which had been re-rendered only a few years ago.

Completely beset with fear that I wouldn't be able to enter rehab, especially after the knee went, I left a message with Lambeth drug and alcohol to see if they'd confirmed with my guy about their guy suggesting for me to reduce my alcohol intake. Later on, the guy I spoke to called back and confirmed that he'd spoken to my guy.

Showers persisted so there was no way I could go around the windows to gloss and touch up. No more black appeared on the basement floor so I went home in a stinking mood.

Only that Monday, I'd looked at the forecast and said to the lady of the house how clear the outlook was for the remaining few days. I'd had such good fortune with the weather till then but I was cocky and joked that God was always with me, if only on the weather front. He'd had the final laugh, spitting in the face of my arrogance.

Since the weekend, I've inadvertently developed a resentment against the lady over trifling issues surrounding meeting her friend for supper last week. She doesn't like it when I insist on a full pint at the pub when we go out, which is hardly ever nowadays, so when my pint came with ice cream on top I was suitably aghast and asked the barman to top it up.

'What? With lemonade?' he said.

I kept my cool but the damage had been done. When we went to sit at a table we got talking and the lady asked whether I considered myself to be a loose cannon, bringing up the issue with the barman. In the first five minutes of finally getting to meet one of her friends, she'd slammed me down to the size of a pea.

After finishing our drinks we went to a restaurant across the road and there was a queue at the door. I was behind her and got talking to the bloke behind me. When she saw me talking to him, the first thing she said when we sat down was 'you weren't arguing with him, were you?' The evening went well after that, though. Both of us wanted a happy time.

I hadn't brought my qualms up since then, causing the resentment to strengthen. To make matters worse, on the Saturday, she'd been at a family member's 55th birthday party and was chatted up by two guys. Did she really need to tell me that? By the Tuesday of the downpour I was fuming and refused to answer her texts.

For the past month or so, she's been adamant that we be kind to one another in the lead-up to my entry into rehab but I wasn't best pleased with her latest version of 'kindness'. When this sort of thing crops up, I tend to zip the lip and let it fester, hoping that it'll miraculously relieve itself over time, which never happens. In the end, I usually mention whatever qualm it is (jealousy) that's resided in my head and she rationalises it out. I know talking helps but I feel like such an unsuitable lover for her that I tie myself up in knots, thinking she'd be better off just assuming she only loves me because I'm a deadbeat who gives her great sex.

As I had to go to Guildford on Thursday, this would be our last chance to see each other before rehab on Monday, apart from Sunday, which would only be brief.

Next day, all I needed to finish the job completely was some more masonry paint for the blemished basement walls. I parked up outside Lords, got it and zoomed over to work for eight. By eleven I'd given a fresh coat to the walls, taped the floor (with careful attention to the knee, which was still aching), painted the black trim and put another coat on the staircase. All that was left to do was pack up my stuff and stick it all in the car. The customer helped me load up and we left on excellent terms.

The lady was ready to be picked up so I drove down to Chelsea. Being still in a huff with her, I greeted her nonchalantly and asked what she'd like to do. That morning, she'd suggested that we just go for lunch somewhere, but she knew what I really wanted; a goodbye cuddle.

There were two sets of ladders going the whole way and over the front passenger seat so I'd made a little space for her beside all the dustsheets on the backseat, which she didn't mind. Wanting to know why I'd been so insensitive to her the last few days, I ignored her and asked where we were going. She said go as if I was going home so I got on my way. After a short time I sheepishly explained the reasons for my upset. I also told her that if we were to depart with kindness I hadn't found her behaviour very inspiring.

She asked me to pull over, got out and tried to sit on my lap in the driver's seat but it was too tight and I was still unresponsive. She gave me a kiss but I couldn't return it. Then she said we should go back to the flat to talk things through so she got back into her little space and I drove off, quietly happy that I'd probably get my cuddle.

I felt better when she apologised. She hadn't meant to hurt my feelings, suggesting that we can both be tetchy and jealous at given moments, and with the slightest push.

'I love the way you are, *who* you are,' she said, 'but you can be such a child. You need to tell me when you're unhappy with me.'

I sighed and then smiled at her in the rear-view mirror, fighting back the tears of a teenager in love.

Famished, we stopped off at the Somalian place for a chicken and rice takeaway and then parked up at home.

She had a few mouthfuls as I gorged on the dish from its aluminium tray. I told her that I'll be getting some tracksuit bottoms for my time in rehab, where I'd have plenty of time to lounge around. She'd already thought of that, though, pulling out a gift-wrapped present and passing it to me. It was a pair of grey trackies so I tried them on. Also from her bag, she plucked out a cashmere jumper and a commemorative hardback edition of her favourite book, *Wuthering Heights*.

All negative thought disappeared instantly. A fool, I'd wronged her for just being herself. We all have foibles and she'd put up with an awful lot of mine in the last year, especially since the move.

We went to bed for a short while and then it was time to take her home, both of us relieved that the tension between us had been dislodged and found peace. When I dropped her off I told her I wanted a pint. She knows better than to complain or try to turn my thoughts around and we parted happily. There's always a massive weight of loss when we part but that's the deal.

I ended up at The Junction and had two beers there with a quick go on the fruity. Romantically thinking this to be my last gamble, I told the barman he wouldn't see me for quite a while and revealed where I was going. By doing so, I knew I'd resigned myself to rehab. But then Kieran called and told me I was a fool, that I'd have my personality gouged out of me. I'd be like a programmed zombie.

'You're fine with a few drinks, mate,' he said. 'All you need to do is open an account at the building society. Look what's it's done for me. I'm up to five eight now.'

Since he'd opened his account with them about a year ago, he'd somehow managed to build up money instead of floating all of it across a bookies' counter. The three-month holding account had proved to be a revelation for him and I'd seen vast improvements in his drinking habits too. Not only had he reduced his usual spree from fifteen pints down to a much more manageable six, those sprees were far less frequent. It was clear that by opening an account and depositing money that I couldn't touch my own financial affairs could be put into similar order.

A few months back, I tried to open an account but the utility bills I took along were insufficient. What they really wanted was my council tax bill. The lady there told me my details were filed so all I had to do was return with the council tax bill and I'd be good to go. Sadly, every time I went down to Guildford I was either working or drinking and gambling so I never made it back. I'd foregone the idea, thinking I'd get all that stuff sorted once I was in rehab.

'They'll turn your brain to mush, mate,' he said. 'I've seen it dozens of times.' He had, too, recalling various gamblers who'd gone in and come out like jibbering wrecks, or so he said.

I turned the conversation back to him and he told me he'd just had two fillings done for two hundred quid so he'd gone to the bookies in a vain attempt to win back the dental costs. It didn't work. All his trap ones had come nowhere and he reckoned one of them had a piss at the finish line. All his horses had either fallen, pulled up or drifted into nothingness. The only vague recompense was a late bet on a horse that ended up having to be put down after falling at the last fence. He'd lost two hundred, which was about right. After that, he paddled about around town and once the anaesthetic wore off he didn't even have enough for a beer. Nothing new there.

Bored of The Junction, I walked to the bookies across the road for another last hurrah but I only stayed for a couple of races.

In one, the horse I'd backed a fiver each-way at 17/2 came a very close second but then there was an announcement that a stewards' enquiry was underway as the winner may have interfered with my horse.

I couldn't hang around because the meter had just run out on the car so I cashed it in as an each-way bet (thirteen quid) and said I'd be back to collect my winnings if the result was reversed. The young female server smirked and said nothing.

Lo and behold, when I got home and checked, my horse,

Direct Security, had been announced the winner, with Harry's Heroes demoted to second place. I got back in the car and drove to Clapham with trepidation, imagining the excuses they might come up with not to pay out.

When I got there, the server who'd taken my slip and paid out each-way had gone. The young female who had been next to her had taken over to tend the place alone for the evening shift. She told me that I'd cashed out as an each-way and that it had been settled. Nothing more could be done. Protesting, I felt my anger rise so I took my jumper off and tied it around my waist.

A guy came up to the counter and told me that someone had the same horse but he'd bet on a machine. It had been settled as a win and paid out without a problem. I told the server but she was playing dumb by then.

Because there's no telephone service for servers to call up and settle issues any more, they have to message 'advisors' online, so after some harsh words she eventually decided to start a 'conversation' on the messaging service at her till. I'd already shown her on my phone that the online results platforms, Timeform and Racing Post, had listed my horse as the winner. Even the results board there at the shop listed it.

After fifteen minutes of tapping away on her keyboard she said I could have a paltry twenty quid as it had been a dead heat, according to the advisor. This was a lazy lie, hoping I'd go for it without fuss. I refused and she started tapping away again.

Other gamblers came up to the counter to place bets but they were told to wait while she sorted my problem out. One got shirty with her and a loud debate got underway, ending with her swearing at him. He waddled off, scared he'd be kicked out if he carried on. By this time, no one could place bets and the server was getting hot under the collar. She said the advisor was an idiot. She'd cut off her link after trying two or three more lies to get me off the server's back. They were becoming increasingly outlandish and I couldn't help laughing. I'd wait it out, if only for the journal.

After about half an hour I asked her to look for my ticket so I could take it and retrieve my winnings the next day at a different Paddy Power. I'd give her back the thirteen quid so she could make the ticket active again.

With a worried look on her face, she started looking through all the tickets of the last few hours but she couldn't find it so she passed me the pile and I did a second check. The ticket wasn't there. Funny, that.

At this time the server announced that she couldn't take the stress. This whole debacle was playing havoc with her OCD. I asked her to calm down, that we'd get to the bottom of it one way or another. She said thanks and her manner changed. I asked for a copy of my ticket from the database and she did that quick enough, sliding it across the counter for me to take. I stuck it in my wallet and told her how this shitstorm would make for excellent reading in the gambling journal I was writing.

That was when she got on the phone to make a call.

'I thought you had to use the messaging service.'

She frowned, putting the phone on speaker for me to listen to the automated voice asking her to wait. 'It'll take about twenty minutes for someone to answer, guaranteed. They want us using the messaging service.'

She gave me a frown, with half a smile.

Now that we were on the same side I felt sure that the issue would be resolved, and after about half an hour someone answered and told her to pay me forty-seven pounds and fifty pence.

When she passed over the cash she said sorry again and again. I told her not to worry, it would take me longer than the two hours I'd waited to write the episode in the journal. Paddy Power's shenanigans would be known, but they're all the same, nasty little shysters using vulnerable people on both sides of the counter.

I got up at about six the next morning to get to the job in Bramley for eight, driving down the A3 and stopping off for coffee and a sandwich.

When I got there I hardly recognised the place because they'd built a garage at the front and given the porch a new look with oak posts. It turned out that they'd wanted to move but the stamp duty would have set them back a hundred grand so they ploughed it into the house instead.

Sophie's an old client who's always been decent with me. It had been at her house that I spilt paint on a carpet for the first and only time in my career. I'd tried to clear it up but it wouldn't budge so I raced out and rented a wet and dry vacuum cleaner but by that time the damage was done. She let it go in the end so I offered to do a half-day for free next time round. That was four or five years ago and she's used me a few times since on other jobs.

The new kitchen, which I would be painting, looked great. She said that the cabinet people needed to do a few bits of work but that it shouldn't impede my progress. This always worries me, other trades traipsing about making more work for me as they correct mistakes. I'm the gift wrapper and need to be left alone. All mistakes need to have been remedied.

I put a sheet down on the island and brought my stuff in from the car, then the cabinet people turned up. It was Dere Kitchens, a company I'd worked for as cabinet painter. We'd parted company a few years back when they found someone cheaper.

The main guy was there and he told me his boys wouldn't be long, just a few things needed doing and I'd be left in peace. It's funny because he'd always slate other trades on jobs for not doing their work properly and on time, which put their noses out of whack to complete the work. Now, here he was, playing the same game with me.

I'd quoted Sophie for three days' work and I couldn't go into Sunday because I had to pack for rehab, tidy the flat up and see the lady one last time.

By teatime Dere Kitchens' boys had their stuff all over the place and I had to pick places to work around them. After filling some large cracks I opened a half-full tub of paint I already had and got on with a few areas.

That ran out by lunchtime so I went to get two more big ones from the hardware shop in Cranleigh. I said I'd be about an hour, by which time the boys reckoned they'd be well gone. How many times had I heard that little chestnut?

I went to The Three Horseshoes for a couple of pints. Being a Thursday, the pre-treatment therapist would be calling as usual at three, so when I got a call at three on the dot I thought it would be him and went outside to the much quieter garden to pick up.

The call turned out to be from a woman called Joan at the clinic. She was calling to answer a few questions I had after receiving written confirmation of my entry by email.

First off, I asked if I could come in my car and she said that would be fine. There was a car park at the clinic but they'd have to take the keys from me. With the MOT running out in November I'd wanted to put a new one on there, then sell it and buy a nice little petrol banger. That way, I'd have a ULEZ compliant car ready to roll for when I got back from Barbados. Trouble was, if they had the keys I wouldn't be able to sell it.

It was far worse news when I was told that I couldn't bring my laptop. I tried to reason with her but she wouldn't have it.

'You'll have to write with a pen and paper,' she said. 'It'll be OK once you get going.'

Also depressing was the reassertion that there could be no contact whatsoever with the outside world for the first fortnight there.

'That includes writing letters,' she said.

This registered as an ominous request and I started thinking they'd drug me up from the start, just like the last place, turning me into a dribbling zombie by the end of the fortnight.

I kept cool and said I'd see her at the clinic on Monday at about 2pm.

The therapist called directly afterwards for our final telephone session. We'd talked every Thursday at three for the past four months and this, he said, was my send-off call to wish me all the best at the clinic. He'd talked with Lambeth and all was fine with my reduced alcohol intake.

After that I got the tubs of paint and raced back to the job but the boys were nowhere near finished so I got on with what I could. They eventually fucked off at four, saying one of them would be back in the morning to do a few extra things.

When I left at six I saw one of my dust sheets on the patio so I went to take it inside but it was full of their crap, which went all over the place, a final kick in the teeth to end the day.

Trying not to seem too perturbed, I said bye to Sophie and she said sorry for the boys being there. I told her it wasn't her fault and that I was still on for a Saturday finish.

I stayed at my sister's place down the road that night and we had a curry with her husband. I talked about my fears of going to rehab and also of the news that my daughters' identities were almost impossible to find. A friend of the lady, who's good with ancestry, couldn't find any records for them. Both of my daughters have had two name changes. In thirteen years their mother hasn't sent even one photograph of them to me.

I got up bright and early the next day and tried to make a bacon sandwich but I couldn't work out how to turn on my sister's new hob so I had to settle for a ham sandwich.

At work, I got going and then the cabinet boy rolled up at nine. I asked how long he'd be and he said a few hours so I started doing little areas around him.

To do the ceiling of a large kitchen, the place has to be completely clear for a good path, and sheeted up. Painters start at the top and work their way down, much the same as in life, so ceilings are always first for the paint.

By lunchtime he was still naffing about all over the place, tools strewn. I opened a tub of paint and found it to be too watery so I went back to Cranleigh to replace it, via The Three Horseshoes. I had three quick pints, worrying that I wouldn't be able to give the ceiling its first coat later on. I didn't want to risk doing both coats the next day because it can peel off in areas if it's not completely dry and that's the whole thing screwed. I'd prepped it to perfection.

With the old lager bravado added to my pent-up anger I lost one-sixty on the new machine at the pub and then felt like getting my own back at the bookies so I strolled into Cranleigh, quickly taking another sharpener at the pub opposite.

That morning, I'd opened up to Sophie about rehab when she brought me a cup of coffee and she'd been very understanding, showing kind concern. I told her I don't normally open up about my gambling as it scares the crap out of people, especially customers, who might think I'll get the removals people in while they're out for the day. I told her about the journal and she said she'd like to read it.

'It's very sad,' I warned her.

At the bookies I was in a right state and blew a monkey in an hour, two-thirds of my wages down the drain.

When I got back with the new tub, the boy was still there. I finished off one section of the kitchen away from the main part of the room, a sloping ceiling that joined onto walls at a slight angle so that I could do both in one hit. I prepped the laundry room and put a coat on that.

At four, he packed up and said a sheepish goodbye, which I ignored. The main thing was that he'd gone for good so I ploughed on, finally able to sheet up floors and surfaces to apply a first coat to the main ceiling.

As my sister was babysitting overnight at her son's house, Sophie had kindly booked me in at a B and B above a pub in the village. When I said goodbye at about seven, she told me that a plumber was coming the next day to do a few hours at the sink. If it wasn't her I'd have had a wobbly but I kept my cool. She said that she'd compensate me for any extra time spent there but I assured her that I was still on for a finish the next day, be it a long one, which was fine by me. She handed me a twenty and told me to get a nice supper. If I wasn't so in love with the lady I'd have possibly started to entertain thoughts of asking her to come along for a few drinks with me. She's married though. All the best ones are.

Kieran called just as I was leaving so we arranged to meet at The Queen Vic. He'd parked up at The Sea Horse down the road. It's got a nice quiet car park so he likes to sleep in the van there. A few pints and they're sweet enough.

I treated us to pints and jerk chicken with rice and we talked through our latest betting sprees. Regarding rehab he was still adamant that I was making a very bad move.

'They'll fry your brain, mate,' he said.

'Yeah, I've been wondering about that.'

At the B and B pub I threw my bag into the room and then went to the pub next door to be a nuisance. The landlord runs a tight ship, not only because it's well run but because he's a tight git. I had a couple of pints at the bar.

Back at the B and B pub I was dying for a joint and sufficiently pissed to ask a bloke in the garden if he knew anyone. Why the hell would I do that? I was one day away from entering rehab after four months of tough reckoning and here I was, ready to mess it up with a mind-numbing spliff. Luckily it was a no from the guy so I supped up and crashed out in my room.

I woke up the next day with a thumper so I had a shower to wake myself up. I hadn't washed properly since starting the job and my hair was full of dust from sanding down the ceilings and walls. I gave it a good shampoo and felt a lot better but the hangover was a rotter.

I got into work just before eight, resigning myself to the fact that another trade would be along shortly. Sophie made me a very nice coffee and I put a second coat to the laundry room walls, which would need a third coat because of the contrast from its previous colour. She likes everything in white.

At nine the plumber arrived and got going at the sink. Immediately, though, there was a problem. The electrician had failed to put an additional socket behind the sink, which the plumber needed for the new water system.

The plumber came up with an idea, which meant the husband would need to go to Screwfix to get something, so off he went. But then the plumber announced to Sophie that he'd given him the wrong code for the product so she called him but he'd already got the thing. They tried knocking their heads together for another solution, calling around electricians, but the fact was the cabinets were so tightly fitted that nothing could be done until the fitters came back to make room for the electrician to do his work. Also perturbing was that the plumber had been given the wrong attachment for an adjoining pipe. These are the shenanigans of the building trade, one big spinning ball of chaos. The buck can always be passed onto the next trade, and the next, or maybe the supplier. On and on the chaos spins until all mistakes have been corrected.

One thing that kept me buoyant that day was how Sophie and her husband stayed cool with all the new problems at the sink. That sort of goodness really has an impact on me.

The plumber was a decent guy. He didn't move from the sink so I was a pig in shit, tearing around the place like a whirling dervish. Arsenal were playing Spurs in the midday kick-off so I listened to that. We ended up thrashing them 4-1 so I was a happy puppy with an end to the job in sight.

With the last of the skirting boards painted I took up the masking tape and started to pack up. With everything in the car I quickly changed into civilian clothing and Sophie gave me the lion's share of the money in cash. She'd deposited the rest into my account and added a bit extra.

What a lady! She gave me a hug and wished me well.

I had to get to the computer shop by six to return the dud mini laptop and get my sixty quid back so I raced into Guildford and got there just as he was closing up, then I went to Waitrose and bought myself a nice piece of sirloin and some real treats for an evening at home. The last thing I wanted to do was drink after such a heavy night and I had Match of The Day to look forward to.

Back home I had a good soak in the bath with the potatoes and carrots thrown in the oven. Dressing gown on, the lady texted to say she was in a state about not being able to text me for my first two weeks at the clinic. I texted back saying all would be well and that time would fly. I'd make sure she could visit me very soon afterwards. We'd get through this together, one way or another. She admitted that she was only thinking about herself, that I was doing the right thing going in, but she couldn't stand the idea of me being so far away. What the hell she sees in a loser like me I'll never know.

Sunday was a weird one. I'd arranged to go to Notting Hill to pick up a grand in cash that the customer had for me. Also, another sister was in town and staying with a friend in Portobello. We'd arranged to have lunch together but then she texted during Match of The Day to say she had a streaming cold and couldn't make it.

I still needed to go and get the cash so off I went on the tube. Since talking with Joan from the clinic, my overall view of rehab has been hit hard. In this final week of the 28 days' sobriety/reduction, I drank almost every day, rendering the progress made during the first three weeks as good as obsolete.

Also, now that it had been made crystal clear that I couldn't take the laptop in, I knew I wouldn't be able to finish the journal until January, which is a definite no no. Added to that, my levels of trust in authority are shot to bits. I can't help thinking I'm putting myself in a precarious position. With the care system in tatters and horror stories coming thick and fast on Panorama, I do wonder just how vulnerable I'll be cooped up with all the other nutters. Then there's the voice telling me this is an inside job, that only I can pull myself out of the hole. Anyone can scupper recovery but you have to listen to your gut too.

What would the other dozen or so all-male gamblers be like? My guy at the clinic always insisted that I'd have to sign a document that forbade me to retell stories I heard from the other gamblers. Everyone would be made aware that I've been writing a gambling journal, so how would that pan out? At least at home I'm on my own and away from the lunacy. Not being able to put the car through the MOT would be a real kick in the bum too.

I got the cash from the customer and then went to The Castle for a few pints, still seeing this as my last day of freedom, once again paying my respects to the glory of lager. I went around Portobello to look for a present for the lady but it was full of tourist tat, boho crap made to look like the real deal when it's actually made in China by dissident workers in prison. Nothing's real any more.

The lady had spent the weekend with girlfriends in The Fens, something they do every year to talk and walk and drink and eat and laugh together. The plan was to meet her at Kings Cross for one final goodbye. Her train came in at 3.30.

On the way to the tube I saw City playing United at The Elgin so I stopped in for a pint. There was ample time to watch the first half so I had another and then took to the street for the tube. City were all over United.

I hardly ever met the lady with beers on board so I knew my countenance would be received with dismay. Four pints down, my will to rise above the alcohol dissolved and as I got on the tube I knew I'd only make things go badly between us. I almost turned around and went back to the pub.

At Kings Cross I looked up at arrival times and saw her train was scheduled to arrive at four, not 3.30. With that half-hour to kill I went up to the main road and saw that The Euston Flyer had the match on. Just as I got my fifth pint in, the lady texted to say she'd arrived so I drained that and asked her to meet me on the main road by the traffic lights.

She could see I was worse for wear and I felt terrible, but instead of apologising I went into one of my lazy-minded moods.

We scurried down a side street like rats, as always aware of prying eyes and the repercussions for her at home. She only had three quarters of an hour to spare so we ducked into the first place we saw, a Greek bar.

From a little table we ordered drinks (she had a Coke, having drunk all weekend, and I had a Mythos). We talked about things but she could see I wasn't really there. I had two grand to give her for safekeeping while I was in rehab so I passed that over and she put it in her bag. She handed a conker to me, which she'd found in The Fens somewhere. I stuck it in a pocket.

'This is meant to be a loving goodbye and here you are pissed as a fart.'

I just looked at my beer on the table. When we left to go back to the station I played on the cloak and dagger aspect and stayed well behind her as she wrestled with her wheelie bag. At the tube we parted without kissing (that hasn't been an option in public for ages anyway).

Back in Brixton I was keen to carry on drinking so I went to The Ritzy and had two quick pints. I needed to cancel out my shameful behaviour with the lady and the bookies beckoned.

At the Ladbrokes (aka Brokelads), four hundred in cash went straight through Hercules in about half an hour. I couldn't leave it so I asked the server to put a hundred on the machine with the card, scraping back three-twenty.

There was an American race starting up with a horse called

Bad Suzie so I stuck fifty each-way on her but she didn't even make the frame. I left and had another quick one at The Ritzy.

By that time I was seriously lashed. Kieran called to see how I was so I told him about the meeting with the lady but all he wanted to talk about was rehab.

He kept saying 'don't go to rehab, don't go to rehab'.

I laughed it off but he kept saying it so I said bye and hung up. I knew he meant well, these were his thoughts, not mine, or so I thought.

I still hadn't bothered to eat all day but I wasn't ready to go home so I walked down to a cute little bar next to the tube and got talking to a guy outside. He passed me a joint and to my surprise I took it and smoked the rest of it, knowing full well that it would show up in the test results at the clinic.

In the time it took to feel the effects of that joint I knew I wouldn't go. There was Bukowski sitting at the bar holding a thumb up to me, smiling, glad that I'd made the right choice.

I gave the guy a tenner and he passed me a few little buds. I had a dainty little Bukowski jig inside the bar and then caught the bus up the hill, stopping off at the supermarket for a bottle of beer.

Back at the flat I danced around the living room, smoking joint after little joint with music blaring. When I saw that the lady had texted numerous times I threw my phone onto the sofa and carried on dancing, indifferent to the pain I was causing. I didn't even text her good night.

In the morning I knew I wouldn't go. My head was thumping awfully and I was still in an angry, resentful mood with the lady so I texted her saying I wasn't going in and that, instead, I'd find myself a rich woman to live off. It was a callous thing to say and she texted back that I must go, please go, just get in the car and go!

In the end, at about ten, we talked on the phone and I apologised for being such a nasty idiotic fool. She made it clear that I'd overstepped a certain mark to her mind and she didn't know what to say, let alone think.

I called the clinic and Joan called back to see what was going on so I explained my position. She tried to reason with me but I wasn't for budging.

'You're just not ready, that's all it is,' she said, adding that their door was always open and wishing me well.

Once that was done, all I could think of was getting away somewhere hot by the beach so I could write the rest of the journal and put it to bed. Trouble was, I gave the lady two grand yesterday and I've spent the lion's share of what I had left so I couldn't book anything online. I texted her to ask for twelve hundred to be transferred and by midday the money was there.

Looking online, I saw that flights to Crete were cheap and there were some pretty good late season hotel deals.

I won't write about the holiday because it was a shitshow. I ended up going to Corfu.